"I don't care who dies, as long as the dog lives."

Most People

# K-9 RAMBO

## THE DUTCH MASTER

RADA JONES

APOLODOR

This book is a work of fiction. Names, characters, places, and incidents are the product of the author's imagination or are used fictitiously. Any resemblance to actual events, locales, or persons, living or dead, is entirely coincidental.

Copyright © 2022 by Rada Jones

All rights reserved.

No part of this book may be reproduced in any form or by any electronic or mechanical means, including information storage and retrieval systems, without written permission from the author, except for the use of brief quotations in a book review.

APOLODOR PUBLISHING

# K-9 RAMBO

**1**

———

I don't know about you, but I curl with my nose under my tail and catch a nap whenever I'm worried.

My brother Rebel growls, my sister Riot snarls, and Arco barks himself into a mouth-foaming frenzy. But what's the point? I'd rather be sharp and ready when trouble strikes. Like now.

The engine's humming kept me snoozing. But now that it stopped, I can't wait to stretch my legs and empty my bladder.

Arco stirs in his crate. He sniffs so hard he sneezes, then claws at the grate.

"Where are we?"

Good question. I don't get much either, over the truck fumes and the driver's sweat. Still, the air feels weird. It's hot, dry, and dusty, not wet and salty like home. Then the wind changes, and the smell of hot grease hits my nose and makes me slobber.

"Some fast-food place," I growl, hoping someone lets me out before I burst.

"Yeah, yeah, but where?" Arco whines.

"Who knows? Not home, for sure," I mutter as the man who picked us up at the airport opens the tailgate. I can tell it's him by the smell of cut grass and his round ears sticking out like trophy handles.

He glances at Arco, who bares his teeth and barks up a storm.

"Let me out! Let me out right now, you hear me! I can't take it anymore! I've been locked in this crate for hours."

"Yeah, yeah." The man taps the crate, then comes to stare at me.

I stare back.

"Welcome to Texas. How ya doing, pal?"

I wag my tail.

"Fine, thanks. You?"

He does a double-take.

"You OK, Rambo? You want a potty break?"

Arco barks like he's seen the mailman, but the man ignores him and opens my door. I jump out, but my legs are so numb I tumble in the dust.

Oh well. I scramble to my paws, shake, and walk the man to a patch of sorry-looking grass with some scraggly bushes in need of watering. I lift my leg, check the peemails left by all sorts of dogs I've never met, and wonder why these bushes don't look any better after all this watering.

A hundred feet away, monster trucks spew fumes and growl, racing down the road. But they're not my problem. Pooping is.

I follow a young retriever's trail to the right spot under a dwarf pine, spin around three times as per protocol, and make sure I face north before I empty.

"Good boy, Rambo."

Round-Ears slips me a strip of beef jerky and takes me back to my crate to take out Arco, who's still barking.

We get back on the road. I curl in my crate, feeling better now that I'm empty. But Arco doesn't. He sticks his nose through the grate, sniffs the road, and growls for the thousandth time.

"Where the heck are we going?"

I'm tired of telling him I don't know, so I lay my nose on my paws to catch an extra nap. I wake up just as the truck stops again, and I know we've arrived.

"We're there."

"There, where? And how do you know?" Arco growls.

"I smell it."

I've never been here. As a matter of fact, I've never been further from home. But this place smells like grilled meat, grass, and dogs, and I just know it's the end of our trip.

Round-Ears parks on a wide patch of low grass warmed by a mellow sun surrounded by oaks, pines, and a few green bushes. I can't see the house behind them, but I smell people, food, and smoke. And at least a dozen dogs.

Round-Ears returns with a wide man wearing dark glasses and a dog-training vest.

"There they are, Butch."

"How do they look?"

"Beautiful. The Malinois is a bit high-strung, but the Dutch is cool as a cucumber."

"Sure, he's high-strung after staying locked in that crate for sixteen hours. Wouldn't you be? Let's see them."

Round-Ears heads my way, but Butch shakes his head.

"Not the Dutch, Mike. Let's see the Malinois first."

Arco barks like a lunatic while Mike clips a lead to his collar, then jumps out and gets to business, sniffing the men, the grass, and the trees. His head up and his tail held high, he prances like he's working the runway.

Butch scratches him behind his ears.

"You're right, Mike. What a big, handsome boy. Let's see him work."

He takes out a leather pillow tied to a rope and thrashes it around. Arco snaps to attention and leaps to get it, but Mike holds him back. Arco goes mad. He barks and growls, chasing that thing like it's a cat.

Butch smiles.

"Great pursuit and good prey drive. Give him a bit more leash."

Arco sinks his teeth into the leather pillow, and he won't let go. He growls like a chainsaw and holds on to it as Butch grabs it, pulls on it, and tries to shake him off.

"He's got a full, confident bite. Nice grips! Good job, Arco!"

They play tug with that pillow until the man starts panting, and Arco's dark muzzle turns white with foam. The man lets go, and Arco gets the pad to himself to shake and tear apart.

Butch wipes his forehead with his sleeve.

"That's what I'm talking about! I'm not a betting man, but I'd bet you a cold beer against a warm diet lemonade that he'll make an excellent protection dog. He's got great potential. How old is he?"

"They're both thirteen months old," Mike says.

"And no training, other than the basics?"

"Right."

"Well, you can see his genes at work. Great. Put him away, and let's see the Dutch."

Mike clips my leash and takes me out. Butch nods.

"Another handsome boy! Golden brindle all the way but for the dark face and ears. Just look at how he holds his head and tail! This one's gonna go like hotcakes!"

"Really? I thought it was all about the training."

"That's BS. They all say they want a serious protection dog and Schutzhund and yada-yada, but in the end, it all comes down to looks. Looks shouldn't matter, but they do. Every soccer mom I've ever seen will take a big, handsome dog like this over the best-trained mutt in the world. And, truth be told, few ever get to find out how good their dog really is. Just having a dog like this with you will keep away the riff-raff. Let's see him work."

He throws the leather pillow. I sniff it.

It's soaked with Arco's slobber, and it smells like a hundred other dogs. This guy has played this trick, thrashing this dead thing around like it's alive, with every dog in a hundred miles.

Oh well. I don't mind playing tug, but maybe later. Right now, I want to find out about this place. So I ignore the pillow to sniff the brush. Oops! A cat was here. A Siamese, to be precise. I love Siamese; they sound like fire engines, and you can always count on them being ready for a fight.

Mike pulls me back to the leather pillow.

"Come on, Rambo! Come on, boy. Go get it!"

"Get it? What for? What would I do with it?"

I wag my tail and check out a tiny pine tree. Somebody peed on it yesterday, and I know exactly who. It's a German Shepherd. She's a female...

I'm trying to sniff her age when Butch's leather pillow hits me in the head. What the heck!?

I lose my cool for a moment, and I bite it, but I let go as soon as Butch pulls on it. He can have it for all I care.

Butch shakes his head.

"This isn't right. He's a beauty, but he's got no more prey drive than a squirrel. I've never seen one quite like that."

"Can you train it into him?"

Butch purses his lips and looks down his nose at Mike.

"You can't train prey drive, Mike. It's genetic. You either have it, or you don't. You can work with it and improve it, but you need something to start with. Let's see if we can get him aroused."

Butch grabs a whip.

"Yaaa! Yaaa!" he screams, snapping the whip toward me.

I pull back.

"Hey yaaa! Hey yaaa" he shouts, cracking the whip by my ears.

Seriously? He's clearly lost his mind, so I hide behind Mike.

Butch pants.

"What the heck? You can't even get him aroused. I didn't hear a growl out of him! This dog couldn't care less."

"So, what are you going to do?"

"I'll be darned if I know. I'd love to send him back, but it would cost more than he's worth. And I'd ruin my relationship with my best Dutch breeder. He's never sent me a dud before."

He sighs.

"I'll see if there's anything we can do to salvage him. Maybe we can get him to protection level 1? It's gonna take tons of work, but he should still bring more money than if we sell him as a pet."

He thrashes the pillow again. I sit and watch his face grow longer and longer.

"He just doesn't care, darn it. I wish...

His phone rings, and he drops the pillow to answer.

"Loyal K-9s. This is Butch. How can I help you?"

He nods.

"We train protection dogs for corporate and family. We also do tracking and..."

He shakes his head.

"No, I'm sorry. I'm afraid I don't have any explosive detection dogs at the moment."

"Yes, I understand you have a very lucrative contract with that NGO. I'm sorry your other dog died, but..."

"You can't train a dog in six weeks. Yes, we do have the best dogs and the best trainers, but..."

"How much did you say? How long do you need him for? Six months? Maybe a year?"

His eyes meet mine, and he smiles.

"You know, I just can't say no to you. I happen to have this phenomenal Dutch shepherd....

**2**

———

Butch slips the phone into his pocket with a smile.

"That was God's work."

"What was?"

"That phone call, Mike, is what's gonna keep us afloat this winter. With the gas prices climbing and everything slowing down, it was a bit touch and go for the business. Before the Dutch turned out to be a dud, I'd hoped to sell these two on the spot, then charge for their training. But that won't work if I can't make a high-class protection dog out of this one. The Malinois alone won't bring enough money. But God heard me. We're all set. We'll train the Dutch as a bomb dog and lease him out."

Mike cocks his head like a boxer.

"Who will?"

"Who will what?"

"Who'll train him to detect explosives?"

"You, of course. You know I don't have anyone else."

"Oh, no! That work's way behind me, thank you very much. It's been forever since I last touched explosives, which suits me just fine. It's been almost eight years, but I still have nightmares of this."

He pulls up his pants to show a shiny metal leg.

Butch sighs.

"Come on, Mike. You know I have no one else. And you're the best in the business. And we're not talking about getting real! I'm not sending you to the minefields, for God's sake! You'll just walk the dog in the backyard between ropes and teach him to sit when he smells explosives. It's gonna be fun! The weather's good, and…"

"No, no, and no. I can't do it. I'm already plenty busy with the puppies, the breeding bitches, and everything else. And I have a family to look after. Tim's almost three, Madison is five, and they start school in September. Linda's already struggling between them and her job. She told me I need to pull my weight at home; otherwise…"

"But Mike, it's only June. We need to deliver this dog in six weeks. It's gonna be all over by September. You'll have time to take the kids to school; you can even buy them some new stuff. I'll even throw in a bonus, so you can get Linda something nice."

"Linda doesn't need something nice. She needs a new car. The old one is on its last legs."

Butch gasps.

"But Mike, I don't have that kind of money!"

"Of course not. And I don't have that kind of time."

Butch sighs.

"You know what? I'll throw in the down payment. That's the best I can do."

Mike sighs, and I can smell he's wavering. I don't know what they're talking about, but I know it has to do with me, and I can smell that Mike is getting bullied into doing something he doesn't want to. It's the same with dogs; they just don't talk so much. They bare their teeth and bark instead.

Mike scratches his head.

"Let's say I did it. Who will you send with him to the mine-fields? Cause I'm not going even if you buy me a Ferrari. That's where I draw the line."

"Don't you worry. I have six weeks to find a handler — if they even need a handler. For all that I know, they may have their own. Or it could be one of those contracts where they just bring the dogs and hire locals to train them. Either way, it's not your problem. Your only job is to get this dog ready for the minefields in six weeks."

Mike sighs.

"I don't know, Butch. Six weeks is God-awful short. What if the dog's no good? What if he won't learn?"

Butch shrugs.

"It is what it is. I'll make sure we get paid in advance, and I'll get the dog insured every which way from Sunday. If he blows up, we'll buy a new one."

## 3

Mike got me back in the truck, and I didn't get to say goodbye to Arco. I heard him bark behind the trees, chatting to another dozen dogs, and I barked back, but I don't think he heard me over all that ruckus.

I curled with my nose on my paws and watched the dust rise behind the truck. Laying in that crate was getting old. But, before you could bark "Grass-Fed Beef Kibble," the truck hooked a right, drove down a long dirt driveway, and stopped by a sprawling white house shaded by cypresses.

I sniffed, and the scent of manure hit me in the feels, reminding me of home. Other than the dusty dry air, it smelled just like Volendam. But there were no tulips, and the cows were not the same. They were black and brown, not spotted, like self-respecting Friesians.

I watched a massive red bull with twisted horns longer than my tail chew his cud in the field. He glanced at me with a quirky gleam in his eye, and I left myself a mental note: "Be careful where you pee"; then I jumped out.

The black grill by the door called me. It was almost as big as the picnic table but smelled way better, and my belly growled, reminding me I was hungry. I went sniffing for leftovers when the door blew open, and a little girl in a frilly pink skirt ran out and jumped in Mike's arms.

"Daddy, daddy, Cersei has…"

Her eyes met mine, and her mouth fell open.

"What's this?"

"This is Rambo. He'll be with us for a few weeks."

"Mommy! Mommy! Daddy got a new dog!"

A plump woman with a blonde ponytail burst through the door, wiping her hands on her jeans.

"You'd better be kidding!"

Her blue eyes fell on me, and her jaw dropped.

"You aren't kidding! Mike, what's this?"

Mike's smell turned sour with guilt. He put the kid down, then hugged the woman and sniffed her neck.

"You look lovely, Linda! You smell good too!"

He was right. About the smell, that is. She smelled like fried chicken, and that got me slobbering like crazy. But she pushed him away and pointed at me.

"What's this?"

"This is Rambo. He's just arrived from Holland. He'll spend a few weeks with us while I train him."

Linda's hard eyes turned to him.

"We already discussed that, didn't we, Mike? I told you I can't take on another dog."

"But it's just for a few weeks, sweetheart. Butch said…"

She shook her head.

"I can't believe you let him bully you again. What's the point of being his partner if you can't ever tell him no? Doesn't he have enough staff to look after the dogs? You had to bring him here? You know darn well I have too much on my plate. And you're never here to share the burden."

"I'm so sorry, Linda; I'll try to do better. But this is a special assignment. We only have six weeks to get Rambo trained as a bomb dog and get him shipped overseas. And guess what?"

"What?"

"Courtesy of Rambo, you'll get a new car!"

"I'll believe that when I see it."

She stomped back inside. An orange dog shuffled out, followed by a toddler.

The dog smelled me, and her hackles went up. She stopped dead in her tracks to glare at me, but the kid stumbled forward on chubby legs and came to pet me.

"Doggy!"

His cheeks were smeared with chocolate, so I licked him clean. He burst into laughter and fell on his bottom.

Linda cracked a smile, but the dog watched me with wary eyes, and her muzzle wrinkled, showing a flash of white teeth.

She's not happy to see me.

I wag my tail politely and wait.

She inches closer on stiff legs, and I wait for her to sniff my bottom first. This is her home, and she's older. When she's done, I sniff her tail. She's an old girl, and she hurts.

I wag my tail again.

"Glad to meet you, Ma'am. I'm Rambo."

"I'm Cersei. The humans are mine."

"Yes, Ma'am."

"The house too. And the yard."

"Yes, ma'am."

"Where are you from?"

"I'm from Holland. Far away."

"Why are you here?

"Good question. My breeder put me in a crate and loaded me on a plane. When I landed, I met Mike, then Butch. He said I'm here for training."

"For what?"

"Butch hoped to train me for protection, but I failed the tests. So they'll train me to detect explosives."

Cersei snorts.

"Do you know what that means?"

"No, Ma'am."

"That means that you'll go to the minefields to find bombs. You know what bombs are?"

"No, Ma'am."

"They are evil things that blow up and kill you if you don't pay attention. Did you see Mike's legs?"

"I saw one. It was metal."

"The other one's the same. Mike takes them off when he goes to bed, then puts them on in the morning. His real ones blew up years ago in Bosnia. I was just a pup, but my sister Carrie was with him. She didn't make it back."

"I'm sorry, Ma'am. I..."

The little boy grabs my collar.

"Come on, Rambo. We go inside."

I can smell that Cersei doesn't like this, but what can I do? And the kid is the only one here who doesn't seem to hate me. Mike didn't want me, and I can see why. Linda wants nothing to do with me, and the little girl stands by her mom, acting like I don't exist.

The boy drags me in.

Behind us, Cersei growls.

"Careful, Buster. Don't you dare forget: this is my home, and these are my humans!"

How could I forget?

**4**

---

I've sniffed every inch of this place, and I can tell you one thing: a house is nothing like a kennel.

Unlike that darn crate, my kennel in Volendam had plenty of room for me to stretch my legs, lie down, and even roll over. It was made of nice, soft wood that I could chew on if I got bored, but that seldom happened. That place was a hoot — something always happened, and there was always someone to sniff the breeze with. My sister Riot had the kennel to my left and my brother Rebel the one to my right. Arco and his littermates were right across from us, just a bark away. Not counting the humans, who always came by to bring water, clean the kennels, or take someone out for training.

They even took us downtown to get us used to cars, bikes, and people. I slept over at Anja's house a few times to watch TV with her kids. She was the woman who looked after us. But we mostly lay in our crates, sniffing the wind and barking up the news.

But it was nothing like this house. The place is massive — room after room, all so chock-full of stuff you can't get a good run without jumping over a sofa or crawling under a table.

And the odors! The fried chicken is fantastic — no dog worth his kibble would argue with that. Then sugar, sweet vanilla, eggs, and flour tell me something's baking. Then the delicate aroma of lavender soap I adore. But the big white water bowl smells like bleach, and I hate bleach. I don't think much of shampoo either, especially the medicated one that smells like mint. Phew! As for detergent? Don't even get me started.

Oh well. It is what it is.

I lie on the wood-like floors — you can tell they're fake from the driveway — making sure I block the door. It's a shepherd thing — that's the only certain way to keep track of everyone's comings and goings. I check that I'm centered, then lay my nose on my paws and watch the action, wondering how Arco's doing. I hope he's better than me.

Arco and I grew up together. He's a few days older, much noisier, and as high-strung as they come. We played together as pups, then trained together as teens, but I never thought we'd end up together. We're not alike, you see. He's much more like Rebel — never happy unless he's on a mission. Or Riot, who's as high-strung as girls come. But, when the time came, Hendrik, our breeder, chose Arco and me.

"I understand Arco, but why Rambo?" Anja asked. "How about Rebel? Or Riot, for protection work. Rambo is more the quiet type."

Hendrik shrugged.

"I'll keep Riot here. She's beautiful and has a tremendous pedigree. There's no way I could ever find a better breeding bitch. And Rebel's sold already. We'll ship him to Qatar to some sheik when he's done with his training. Rambo's all I've got left from this litter. He'll do just fine. He's handsome and well-tempered and smart enough to learn the rest."

That's how Arco and I ended up here. But he did great on his test while I flunked, so they sent me here. I wonder where he'll end up, and I miss him already.

Arco was the only thing reminding me of home. Everyone else — Mom, Riot, Rebel, Anja, and even Hendrik – is far behind. Oh, how I miss them.

I'm so cold. Even worse, I feel so alone, away from home, and stuck with these people who don't want me. I shiver, but it doesn't help. It's like I've got winter inside, and I'm freezing — not to my paws, but to my heart.

Mike rests his metal legs on a coffee table and types something on his laptop. Cersei lays on the sofa next to him, watching my every breath over the rawhide bone she's chewing on. Linda fusses in the kitchen, sending over delicious smells that make me slobber, as the little girl watches SpongeBob on TV. Even her brother forgot about me as he sits with her.

Oh well. It is what it is.

I stick my nose under my tail to catch a nap. Whether you're sad, lonely, or bored, naps always help. But sleep won't come near me right now.

I sigh again, wishing I was home, when something hissy lands on my head and bites my ear.

I just got attacked by a cat.

## 5

———

Who'd have thought sniffing bombs was easy as pie?

Mike and I spend our days in a vast hangar so clean it doesn't smell. The shiny white floors smell like nothing. The bright white walls smell of nothing. Even Mike smells like nothing after squeezing into a white hooded suit that makes him look like a white rabbit.

The only things that smell are those that shouldn't. The smells are hidden in shiny metal cans lined in rows on the floor. And they're different every day. Some are good, like bacon, dead fish, kibble, or manure. Some, like gasoline, shampoo, or smoke, are not. But there's always some new scent I need to learn. And they never smell good.

Mike calls them "accelerants," "black powder," "TNT," or "plastics." But whatever he calls them, none of them is something you'd want to roll in. But that's not what I'm supposed to do anyhow. All I have to do is sit and point them out.

It's real easy. Fun too, since Mike rewards me every time I get it right. He tried kibble, but I'm not that crazy about food, so he got me a rubber blob he calls a Kong. He throws it, I catch it, and then we play tug. That's way more fun than kibble.

The first time we played tug, Mike scratched his head.

"Rambo, if you like chasing things and playing tug, why didn't you do it when Butch tested you? You can do it just fine. You'd be a great protection dog."

I wagged my tail.

"Not really. I'm not into growling and biting. I'll do it if it's for real — I love chasing squirrels for sport — but that slobbered leather pillow? Why bother? What would I do with it anyhow?"

Mike's heart changed after that. He gave me treats and scratched behind my ears. He even called me on the sofa, though Cersei gave him the stink eye.

Just yesterday, she growled at me to get off so she could take my space. I tried to leave, but Mike held me back.

"No, Cersei. Leave him be. You've had the sofa to yourself all day, and you have plenty of room. Rambo worked hard; he needs to rest too."

Cersei glared at me, but she flattened her ears and curled in the armchair. Linda snorted.

"Don't grow too fond of that dog. He's not here for long."

Mike sighed.

"How could I forget? Butch calls me every day to ask how he's doing. He's counting the days. But Rambo's a natural. He learned all the explosives, from TNT to plastics, and moved from cans to field training in only two weeks. If he keeps it up, we'll be done ahead of schedule."

"Good. I can do with one less dog."

Linda sets a couple of steaming plates on the table. They smell like onions, tomatoes, beef, ancho chilies, and cinnamon. Corn, too. They have chili and cornbread for dinner.

Mike dips his cornbread in the chili, and I swallow my slobber. I know I'll get my kibble when they're done. I even get dinner leftovers when the kids don't finish their food, but tonight they're having a sleepover, whatever that is, so there'll be no chili for me.

"But he's not much trouble, is he?"

"He's no trouble other than getting Cersei bent out of shape. She doesn't like him, and I get it. She's ten years old, and she doesn't need any more excitement. It was bad enough when Tyrion showed up."

Tyrion squeezes through the door as if on cue, meowing to tell the world he's back. He's the color of smoke, no bigger than my head, but he's got the heart of a lion. And he's my friend.

That first day when I lay lonely and dejected, Tyrion jumped me. He hissed and bit my ears, but he was only playing. He slept curled next to me and came back every night after that. At first, I thought it weird to hook up with a cat. But since no one else wanted me...

"Well, Cersei has to learn that the world doesn't revolve around her," Mike says, offering Tyrion a piece of cornbread dipped in chili.

"Cersei's too old to learn. You know that saying, 'You can't teach an old dog...'"

"That's BS. Nobody's too old to learn. Dogs, like all of us, can learn if they want to. So can Cersei."

He takes the last swig of his beer.

"I'm sorry that Rambo needs to go to the minefields. That's a terrible job. He's a great dog, and I wish I could keep him."

"You miss Carrie, don't you?"

"Of course. I miss my legs too, but that's not the point. This dog is gold. Rambo can learn anything and do whatever he sets his mind to do. But those freaking minefields? You can't trust them. And you can't trust the people, either. Most of them don't like dogs. They've never seen working dogs, so all they know are the packs of street dogs they throw rocks at. They don't know dogs; they don't like them and don't trust them. There's no way they'll treat him right."

"Well, it's just for a few months. He'll be back."

"Maybe. But unhappy dogs make mistakes, and their handlers do too. And all it takes is one mistake."

"Sorry, Mike. But I bet Butch will get him a good handler. Did he find anyone?"

Mike shakes his head.

"I don't think so. And I don't even know that he's trying. There's no money in that; the money is all in the dog. And if the dog blows up, he collects the insurance.

**6**

———

Then we moved from the cans to the field. Mike stretched some ropes between trees, and I walked between them, looking for the new odors I'd just learned. But, out there, I had so many other things to smell: cows, horses, and even squirrels chasing each other up the trees. I searched in a grid pattern from one end of the lot to the other, then turned around and started over. And whenever I found explosives, Mike threw my Kong and gave me a few tugs.

"What on earth are you doing?"

I looked up. Tyrion's tail whipped in the branches above, where he lay in wait watching two sparrows fight over a worm.

"Shut up and let him be, you silly cat!" Cersei growled from her sunny spot on the porch. "He's got a job to do. He doesn't need a useless no-good like you to break his focus."

I was so shocked that I missed the cartridge Mike had hidden between the roots of an oak tree, so he turned me back to do it over.

But Tyrion couldn't shut up. He never did, not even when asleep. If nothing else, he purred.

"What on earth are they doing?"

"They're looking for explosives. Rambo sniffs them and points them out to Mike."

"And what does that ball have to do with anything? Why are they fighting over it?"

Cersei finished licking her left paw.

"That's Rambo's reward for finding the explosives. Mike pulls on it to make him feel like he's got a live one. It's fake, of course, but it works."

Tyrion's green eyes dilated.

"How do you know all that?"

Cersei glanced at him down her nose.

"First, I'm not a stupid kitten, like you. And second, I saw it all, years ago, when my sister Carrie trained for the minefields. I was going to be next."

"And were you?"

"Nope."

"Why?"

"Carrie never returned. Mike lost his legs and didn't go back, so neither did I."

Cersei studied her right paw.

"But Carrie wasn't much into the Kong, and neither am I. Gimme a juicy treat any day. But these silly shepherds...."

Tyrion didn't answer. He must have fallen asleep. He's more into napping than into conversation. But I didn't forget.

That evening, after I watched Mike take off his legs and lean them against the wall, I went to Cersei. She lay with her nose on her paws by Linda's side of the bed, and I curled next to her.

"I'm sorry about your sister."

Cersei cracked open one eye.

"Tell me about her and Mike."

"Carrie and I had the same mother. We were both the pick of the litter one year apart, so she was ahead in her training. But when she came home, she always taught me the tricks she'd learned. 'Pay attention to the wind, Cersei. It's fickle and wants to trick you. If the bomb is downwind, he'll smell you first, and that's a no-no.' She was kidding, of course. Bombs can't smell. But they do blow."

Cersei sniffed. "I always wondered if the bomb that got her was downwind."

"She sounds like a great dog."

"She was. I was devastated, and so was Mike. I still wonder if Mike was more upset about losing his legs or losing Carrie. It took him forever to get himself together. Linda was his girlfriend at the time, and she helped. 'I never loved you for your legs. As a matter of fact, the new ones smell better,' she said.

"I didn't know what she was talking about — Mike's new legs were metal. They hardly smelled at all. But she stayed with him, and so did I. It took him forever to move from the wheelchair to the crutches, then the cane. It took him even longer to stop screaming every night. Linda said his PTSD gave him nightmares, whatever that means. But we somehow got him back together.

"And now you had to come and turn everything upside down. Mike has been through a lot. He doesn't need to remember the minefields and losing Carrie and his legs. He grieved long enough, and so did I. I thought it was over, but you came, and we started over."

I flatten my ears in shame, though this isn't my fault. I didn't ask to come and train for explosive detection or go to the minefields. The humans gave me no choice.

"I'm sorry."

Cersei sighs. "Me too."

**7**

———

The day Mike opened the door to the passenger seat to invite me into the truck, I couldn't believe it. I always rode in my crate in the back, but now I got to stick my head out the window. It was fantastic! I got to see everything rushing toward us, but even better, I got to smell everything without even sniffing.

All sorts of great scents jammed into my nose at forty miles an hour. Cows, and horses, and chicken, and...dogs? I sniffed again. Yep.

We got to Butch's place.

When I sniffed Arco, I almost jumped out of my skin. I hadn't seen him since the day we landed, and that was so long ago I'd lost count. But now there he was, growling like a chainsaw and tearing down that filthy leather sleeve.

I knew precisely when he caught a whiff of me. He dropped the pillow and dashed to the truck, whipping his tail like crazy and barking up a storm.

"Rambo! Rambo! Rambo! It's you! Boy, it's good to have you back! Where were you? You missed all the fun! I'm almost done with bite work. Butch said we'll start working with the boogeyman! I get to fight decoys, whatever those are, and I can bite them all I want! Isn't that awesome? But don't worry, I'll show you the ropes and teach you everything. First, the bite. You need to bite hard and deep with your full mouth. You hold it with your back teeth and never let go! See?"

He grabbed the leather pillow and shook it so hard I worried his neck would come unhinged. But it didn't, and I was glad that sleeve shut him up. I'd forgotten how wired Arco can get.

I sighed with relief.

"Good to see you're having a good time, Arco."

"The best time ever," he growled around the leather sleeve.

Butch came to check me out.

"He looks good. How's he doing?"

"Fantastic. Rambo's a natural. He's not fast, but he's the smoothest bomb sniffer I've ever seen. Not nervy at all. Never goes back on his tracks, never slows down, never misses. He's a machine, this one."

"I'm sure glad to hear that. Nice job, Mike. I'm shipping him tomorrow."

"Tomorrow? But who's going to handle him?"

"They don't need a handler. I'm leasing him to DOLCO, the Dog Land-Clearing Organization. They're in Cambodia, building a new program from scratch. They'll send half a dozen dogs and a couple of trainers who will train local handlers on site."

Mike's jaw fell.

"I don't like that, Butch. You said you'd get him a decent handler. Now you're sending a rookie dog to train a rookie handler in the minefields? That's a recipe for disaster if I ever saw one."

Butch shrugged.

"What do you want me to do? That's their program. They don't want to just go there and clear a few mines; they want to help the locals do it themselves. And that's way better if you ask me. Those folks have enough land mines to clear for a few lifetimes. No NGO can stay there that long."

"But then they should start with experienced dogs, not Rambo."

"Yeah? And where would they get them? You know as well as I do that everyone, from the TSA to the army, needs explosive-sniffing dogs these days. And there just aren't enough of them. You said the dog's great. Then let him do his job."

"He's great, but he's just a pup! And you want to send him all alone to the other end of the world?"

"Come on, Mike. You're growing soft in your old age! He's just a dog! And he won't go alone. I'll send Frieda with him."

Mike turned purple.

"Frieda? Are you kidding? That dog's nine years old! After walking a mile, her hips get so tight she starts to shuffle. And her eyes are giving up too! She needs to retire!"

Butch laughed.

"Come on, Mike. One's too young. The other one's too old! Get over it, will you? They're working dogs, not babies, for God's sake! They need to work; that's what they're for! If I listened to you, you'd keep them all here forever, and we'd live on Spam and crackers! We have a business to run, and these dogs are our assets. They need to work and bring in income."

"But you've got to give them a flying chance! You'll send an old dog who can barely walk and a rookie who's never seen action without anyone to look after them in one of the most dangerous places on earth? That's crazy! They'll never make it back!"

"Don't be such a party pooper, Mike! They'll do just fine! They're dogs; they can look after themselves. And if they don't make it back — oh well. They're both insured for all they're worth and then some. We'll just have to replace them. We'll buy more dogs and train them. That's what we do."

"But..."

"No 'but.' That's that. And, by the way, the Belgian looks great too. Good bite, good drive, fast learner. I couldn't be more pleased. I called the breeder to order three more: two males and a female. With these two gone, we'll have room to train more. And now that you got back into explosives training, we can expand our offerings. Bomb dogs are hotter than hotcakes these days."

"But you said Rambo was a one-time deal."

"I did. And he was. But there'll be others in the pipeline. Come on, Mike. Remember what this is about. Think about all the lives these dogs will save. They'll save people's lives. Kids' lives. Not only from bombs but from starvation. They'll clear the fields so people can grow food. They'll clear the roads so kids can go to school. Think about all those people who'll get to have their lives back! Isn't that worth a couple of dogs?"

**8**

———

As we drove back, a wild gust of wind blew out of nowhere, chasing the clouds like a flock of ragged black sheep. Swirling around like soot flakes, the blackbirds screamed their anger. The trees shivered.

I curled in my seat, watching the trees dart backward. Seeing Arco was good, but leaving him felt even better. I could do with some peace and quiet, I thought, when Mike's rancid smell hit my nose.

He stank even worse than that first day he took me home and had to confront Linda. I wondered why. Was it me?

But he patted my head.

"You'll be OK, Rambo. Cambodia is not like Afghanistan. And Frieda's a great girl. I trained her too when she was just a pup. I love that dog!"

He choked and went quiet but kept his hand on my shoulder.

The first raindrops fell just as Mike opened the door. The smell of beef, onions, peppers, and ketchup hit my nose, screaming meatloaf.

I licked my drool and crawled under the table. Linda came in with two steaming plates.

"Just in time. Dinner, everyone."

The kids rushed in and hugged Mike's legs. He kissed them and helped them to their seats.

Cersei squeezed under Mike's chair, and we settled to listen to the song of the forks clanging against the plates.

"How's everything?" Linda asked.

"OK. Rambo's leaving tomorrow."

"Really? Where to?"

"Cambodia."

"Did Butch find him a handler?"

"No. He said they'll train the locals."

"Well, that may be for the best. Sorry, Mike, I know you like that dog, and you're worried, but you can't do everything for everybody. Those people need to learn to help themselves."

"That's what Butch says. He says that the dogs will help the Khmers reclaim their lands and their lives. He talks like he's this big humanitarian, but he only does it for the money."

"Well, there's nothing wrong with that. Money matters. Butch has a business to run and kids to feed. And so do you. He does what he has to do."

"I know. Still, there are things that matter more than money. He's not only sending Rambo; he's sending Frieda with him. And there's really no excuse for that. That old dog earned her retirement."

"Sorry, Mike."

Kids chatter. Forks clatter. Jaws chew.

A piece of meatloaf lands by my nose.

I wait for Cersei to gulp it, but she pretends she doesn't see it, so I inhale it. Then I worry.

Something isn't right if Cersei let me have it. But what?

Maybe she didn't see it? Her eyes got cloudy, and she can hardly see after dusk. She almost tumbled down the steps the other night.

No way! Her eyes may be bad, but her nose is as good as ever.

I'm still pondering this when Mike pushes his chair away.

"This was delicious, Linda, but I'm not that hungry. You mind if I let the dogs have the rest?"

"Suit yourself."

Cersei and I inhale the meatloaf — it smells great, though it's a bit heavy on the ketchup. Mike heads to the door.

"Where are you going?"

"I'll take the dogs for a walk."

"In the rain?"

Mike shrugs.

"They don't mind it. And neither do I."

"Daddy?"

"Yes, sweetie?"

"Can you drive me to soccer practice? The other girls' fathers always take them on Saturdays."

"Not tonight. Next weekend, OK?"

"Why not tonight?"

"Because this is Rambo's last night with us. I want to spend some time with him and say goodbye."

Linda slams her glass on the table.

"Rambo will be back, Mike. It's been months since you took Madison to soccer. The other kids are asking if she's got a father."

"I'll take her next week."

"Unless you have something better to do, as usual."

"Linda!"

"What? There's always something. Work. A fence to mend. A dog to train or say goodbye to. You know, Mike, I sometimes wonder if you love the dogs more than you love your kids."

"How can you say that, Linda?"

"Easily. As for me, I don't even have to wonder. I already know."

Mike and I took a long walk in the rain. I inhaled the scent of mud and manure and loved the softness of wet dirt under my paws. I stepped in every puddle until I found a mudhole, and I took a good, long bath.

When we got home, the rain had stopped, and Linda's car was missing.

Mike sat on the bed and took off his left leg, then the right. He leaned them against the wall as usual.

Then he put his face in his hands and cried.

## 9

———

It was still dark when Mike let me out the next morning. My belly growled, but I couldn't eat a single bite. The stench of misery turned my stomach. Mike, Linda, and even Cersei smelled like doom. All but Tyrion, who still smelled like a cat.

Mike lifted my crate in the truck and sent me in as Cersei watched from the door.

I waved my tail goodbye. I wanted to lick Cersei's nose, but she closed her eyes like she was asleep and covered her nose with her tail, so I let her be and jumped in the crate.

Tyrion followed. But before you could say "wild-caught tuna," Mike grabbed him by the scruff of his neck and threw him out.

Tyrion hit the ground hissing. He glared at Mike, then turned to me.

"Where are you going?"

"I dunno. Somewhere where there are mines."

"What are mines?"

"I'm not sure. I just know they stink."

Cersei opened one eye.

"Don't try to find out. All you need to do is keep away. And remember what I told you: Don't get caught upwind. You want to smell bombs before they smell you."

I wanted to thank her since that was the only caring thing she ever told me, but the truck took off, so I sighed and curled in my crate. Once again, I had left behind everything I knew, and I didn't like it one bit. And leaving Tyrion made me sad, even though he was a cat, and I still couldn't wrap my mind around befriending a cat.

The truck stopped, and Butch loaded an empty crate next to mine.

"Everything OK?"

Mike nodded. Butch turned to someone on the ground.

"Get in."

A shaggy gray shadow flew in, and Butch locked the crate. Mike slammed the tailgate, the engine roared, and just like that, we were on our way.

Oh well. I sniffed the other crate out of habit. I felt like I already knew Frieda from everything that Mike had said. But I was wrong.

Frieda smelled neither young nor cheerful, but she was fearless. Unlike me, she had no worries about what was coming.

"Hi, Frieda."

She stuck her nose through the grate and sniffed my way.

"Who are you?"

"I'm Rambo."

"Dutch shepherd, eh? How old?"

"Almost two."

"Dog help us; you're just a pup. Your first mission?"

"Yes."

"Oh well."

She curled, stuck her nose under her tail, and closed her eyes. She looked asleep, but I could smell her thoughts over the truck's fumes.

"How about you?"

"This is my ninth mission. I thought I was done, and I was

looking forward to lying on the sofa and playing ball with the kids, but I guess it wasn't meant to be. And, truth be told, I don't mind work. Retirement is boring."

"Frieda, tell me: How is it out there?"

"Out where?"

"Wherever you've been."

"I've been everywhere. Bosnia, Lebanon, Zimbabwe, Cambodia — you name it, I've been there."

"So, how is it?"

Frieda sighs.

"Mostly hot. I wish they'd send me somewhere cool for a change, but they never do. Wherever I go, it's always hot and full of flies."

"So, what will we do when we get there?"

"Just what Mike taught you. We'll sniff the fields, the roads, and the buildings looking for UXOs — unexploded ordinances — whether they're mines, bombs, or whatever else can blow up and kill you. Whenever you smell something, you point it out to your handler; they take care of it, then you go look for more. Little by little, you clear a patch of land, then move on to the next."

She stopped to scratch her right ear. That got me itchy, so I started scratching too. Scratching is like yawning. It's hard to see someone itching without catching it too.

Frieda sniffed the paw she'd stuck in her ear. She licked it thoughtfully as if trying to discern the subtle flavors of a gelato, then looked at me.

"Listen, kid. I gave you the official line, but the reality is more complicated. Wherever we're going, it's nothing like home. Beyond bombs, there are fleas, mange, and rabies. That's why we don't get chummy with the local dogs. You won't have much of a chance anyhow since they aren't friendly, and you won't be running loose. They keep you on a lead while you work, then lock you in for the night. But you may see them at times, and you'll surely smell and hear them since they're always hungry, and they come close when they smell food."

That doesn't sound too good, so I try to think happy thoughts.

"Speaking about food. What will they feed us?"

"Mostly kibble. They may stir in some add-ons to make it tastier. Or not. Sometimes they don't feed you at all. My friend Lara returned from the Middle East just fur and bones. She said they only got fed every other day."

"Why?"

"They forgot. Or they didn't have enough food. Who knows? Her partner Eli was so hungry he ate something he found in the field. It turned out to be poisoned bait, and it took him three days to die."

My stomach flops. I hope this isn't true, but I bet it is. I know Frieda isn't lying; I'm just hoping her friend was wrong. But my heart tightens, and I wonder if maybe I should have chased that stinky leather sleeve. I'd be at Butch's now, shooting the breeze with Arco, instead of going to someplace where they starve you to death. Unless they poison you.

Frieda smells my worry.

"You OK, kid?"

"Fair to middling. You?"

"Well, pup, if there's one thing I learned in my deployments, it is that worrying doesn't help. It ruins your sleep and messes up your focus. That's no good. Leave that to the humans. They don't know any better. You're a dog, therefore superior. Don't forget you can't control the humans, the weather, or the food. The only thing you can control is you. So take control. Sleep when you can, eat when you find it, and live every day like it's the last. You may just get to live as long as me if you do."

Seeing that she's going where I am at her age, that's hardly enticing. But the last thing I want to do is hurt her feelings.

"Thanks, Frieda. I'll do my best."

She wags her tail.

"Good. One last thing: The only thing just as important as looking after your humans is looking after your partner. You and I, we'll have each other's back. That way, if we're lucky, we may both come back alive. Got that?"

"Yes, Frieda."

**10**

———

What a farking long trip! After Dog knows how long on the plane, Frieda and I got carted to a truck, another plane, and another car. By the time a short man with dark hair sticking out like he'd stuck his fingers in a socket let me out, I felt like I was born in that crate.

I crawled out and sniffed the air. Frieda did too, and after traveling together like forever, we got to sniff each other's bottoms in a proper introduction before looking around.

The place had magic. The humid night was rich with so many new scents they got me dizzy. Someone's scream split the air, then another. Birds, I wondered? A dangling bulb bathed us in harsh light, but beyond that, the night was thick, dark, and mysterious. A gust of wind whipped down the slender stalks around us, and they bent like grasses, rustling their long, sharp leaves. A raindrop fell on my ear, then another. I opened my mouth to catch them.

Frieda sighed with relief.

"Cambodia. The wet season."

"What do you mean?"

"That's where we are, kid. You smell the rotting leaves, the decay, and the smoke?"

"Yes."

"It's the wet season. It rains every day. When it stops, everything turns dry and dusty. But for now, we're in luck."

She shook to arrange her coat, then gulped some dark water from a puddle. I lifted my leg over a fleshy wet plant, but the smells distracted me. Frieda wrinkled her nose.

"A Belgian Malinois. Not one, two. Crickets! You can't sniff your own butt these days without stumbling over one of these neurotics. I remember when it was just us, the German shepherds. Oh well. At least you know who you're dealing with."

We'd just started exploring the darkness when someone barked. Frieda answered, and before you could say "Milk-Bone," two Malinois leaped out of a shelter covered in dry leaves.

"Hey, hey, hey, look who's here! Welcome, guys!" the smaller one barked, sniffing our way. Her ears perked up, and her tail went a mile a minute as she offered her butt to Frieda in introduction. The second one followed.

They came to me, and I let them sniff to their heart's content; then I got my turn. They were four years old and kin, with dark faces, sharp ears, and shiny tan coats. They were friendly but not calm, and they couldn't contain their excitement.

"I'm Frieda. This is Rambo."

"Good to see you guys. I'm Greta. This is Gogol. We're from Bosnia."

"Really? I heard about your breeding program, but I never met anyone. How's it going?"

"Going good. This is our tenth year. We're breeding, training, and sending dogs all over the world for explosive detection. Malinois, of course. The best dogs on earth."

Frieda smiled, showing a perfect set of fangs, and wagged her tail left.

"Rambo and I may beg to differ, but that's not important right now. How long have you been here? How is it?"

"We landed yesterday. It looks good, but for the heat. I've never been that hot, not even in summer. But it rains like all the time, and the mud's terrific!"

"Is this your first job?"

"No. We were in Angola last year."

"Did you like it there?"

Greta shook from the top of her black nose to the tip of her brown tail.

"Not much. The humans were weird. They were like afraid to touch us. And they kept us locked in our crates whenever we didn't work. No outside privileges like here! This whole yard is ours to run in. They don't even lock us in at night. It's awesome! There's always something to sniff, chase, or chew on."

Greta was right. That yard, fenced with slender sticks braided into each other, was big enough for a good run, and the ground smelled like fresh mud and crawled with things I'd never smelled before. The air was warm, humid, and heavy with strange scents that made me drool.

"What's that smell?"

"Prahok. Fish paste. They let the fish ferment in the sun, then grind it into a paste and add it to the food."

A strip of clear drool dripped off Frieda's muzzle. She licked her lips.

"How's the food, by the way?"

"Kibble."

"Just plain kibble?"

"Sadly."

"Speaking of food," Gogol growled.

The gate opened to let in the man who brought us in, carrying a bucket, followed by a slight woman with short hair so blonde it looked white. She looked at us.

"They all arrived? How do they look, Vithu?"

"OK."

Vithu poured kibble into bowls, and we dug in.

The woman frowned.

"Just plain kibble, like that? No water, no supplements?"

Vithu shrugged. The woman shook her head.

"We'll have to work on that. In this climate, the dogs need the best possible nutrition to stay healthy and do their work. A sick dog won't focus on his work, and a dog that doesn't focus is in danger. So is his handler. If your dog looks for food instead of explosives, you're in trouble."

She came closer to inspect us. Frieda caught her eye.

"Hello, old girl. How's it going?"

She rubbed Frieda's ears, then ran her hands over her back, hips, and legs and checked her paws one by one.

"Hips hurt, eh? The back too. Oh, baby girl! You should be home, lying on the sofa, not here looking for bombs."

She moved on to Greta, then Gogol before coming to me.

Her hands were soft but firm and smelled like lavender. She checked my back and bent my elbows. She was just parting my lips to see my teeth when the gate opened, and a tall man strutted in.

"Hi, Ash. Sorry, I'm late. I got chatting with the boys and lost track of time. How do they look?"

Ash wiped her hands on her khakis.

"So-so. That old girl's got bad hips. She should be retired, not looking for bombs. And this one here's just a pup. He can't be much more than a year old; I can't imagine how he could be done with his training. The Malinois look OK. We'll have to see how they work. And they all need better food than plain kibble."

"OK. We'll take care of that tomorrow. Come on, I'll buy you a beer."

"But Brian, don't you want to check them out?"

"What for? You checked them already."

"But don't you want to get to know them?"

Brian laughed.

"I'll have all the time in the world to know them way better than I want to. Let's go; the guys are waiting, and meeting them is more important than looking at a bunch of dogs."

**11**

———

I was bone-tired, but I couldn't sleep that night. Curled in my crate, I listened to the rain drum on the dry-leaves roof. When it stopped, the jungle came to life. Secretive things I couldn't see whirred, scurried, and slithered in the night. The warm wind carried peculiar scents of creatures watching us from the dark. Then someone screamed, and my hackles went up.

"What was that?"

"Nothing, just the elephants. Go to sleep."

Frieda turned to her other side and started snoring, but I couldn't. The strange scents and the weird calls got my feet all itchy and my heart pumping. I couldn't wait to explore.

The sky went from black to navy, then purple, and the darkness faded. When an enormous red sun floated up, Vithu came to pour kibble in our bowls, then squatted against a palm tree to watch us eat.

"What's he staring at?" Gogol mumbled between mouthfuls of food. "Hasn't he seen dogs before?"

Frieda licked her bowl clean.

"Sure, he has. But not like us. The dogs here don't work, other than maybe watching houses. They roam the streets scavenging for food and run away when someone picks up a stone. They're afraid of humans. Maybe because they eat them."

Greta choked on her food.

"They what?"

"They eat them. Here, dogs are food. Like pigs, sheep, and cows."

My stomach knotted.

"Are you kidding?"

"Nope. Around here, food is hard to come by. People eat whatever they can get their hands on — birds, crickets, worms..."

"Sure, I'd eat that too if I was hungry enough. But dogs? Really?"

"Yep. Old folks say dog meat is good for their health. Especially black dogs. And..."

The gate opened, and Frieda went quiet, thank Dog. My stomach twists and I wish I could unhear all this, but I can't. From now on, I'll never look at Vithu without wondering if he's planning how to cook me.

Ash and Brian come in with two women and a man looking like Vithu's siblings. They're all short and slim, with straight dark hair and white grins splitting round brown faces.

They watch us eat, and I can't help but sniff for dog meat on their breaths. But, thank Dog, I only smell fish sauce and ginger.

Brian clears his throat.

"Now that we're all here, let's introduce ourselves. I'm Brian. For fifteen years, I've trained explosive-detecting dogs in Bosnia, Egypt, Afghanistan, and Angola. DOLAC, the Dog Land Clearing organization, sent us here to start Cambodia's own explosive-detecting K-9 program. We're here to train you to work with the K-9s to clear mines. We'll start with these four, but then you'll train your own dogs and then other handlers. You four are just the first seeds of a program that aims to clear every mine in Cambodia. I dare say we're here to make history, and I'm proud to be part of this. Ash?"

"Hi, everyone. I'm Ashley. I worked with dogs for more than ten years, but this is my first training mission. Brian and I are so proud to start this program that will clear your country of UXOs, and help you reclaim your land. You should be proud too. You four were chosen from hundreds of qualified applicants to be the nucleus of this program. Not only because you speak English, but because of your motivation, work ethic, and excellent recommendations. We're glad to have you. Vithu?"

"Hello, everyone. My name is Vithu. I'm married with two children. I used to teach English, but I couldn't pass it up when DOLAC offered me this opportunity. Bo?"

Bo is a woman. Her long, straight hair is gathered in a ponytail so black it looks blue, and her voice is so soft I need to prick my ears.

"I'm Bo. My husband and I were rice farmers, but one day, as he built a fire in the backyard one day, an unexploded mine blew up in his face. He burned his hands and lost his vision, so he could no longer work. I became the only breadwinner, as he looks after the children, but I couldn't work the farm alone. That's why I applied for this job."

"I'm sorry, Bo. But we're glad to have you," Ash says.

"Chan?" Vithu turns to a girl dressed in yellow with narrow eyes slanting to her temples.

"I'm Chan. I'm eighteen, the youngest in my family. A few years ago, my older brothers found a bombie in the field, and they played football with it until it exploded. One was killed, and the other couldn't walk anymore. To help my family, I had to take a job, so I came to clear mines. But I'm afraid of dogs."

She lifts her shirtsleeve to show the ugly dark scars on her arm.

"I was four when a pack of dogs attacked me. My brothers rushed to save me. Otherwise, I wouldn't be here."

Brian frowns. "What's a bombie?"

"It's a round bomb that looks like a ball. When they find them, kids don't know any better, so they play with them," Vithu says.

Ash touches Chan's shoulder.

"Don't worry, Chan. We'll work through this. These dogs are nothing like those in the street. They're well-trained working dogs, and they won't hurt you. We'll teach you to work with them."

Brian scratches his head.

"I don't know, Ash. Dogs know when you're afraid of them, and they don't like it. They'll take advantage of it. But here's what I don't understand. How did they let you in the program if you're afraid of dogs?"

Chan looks down. Vithu laughs.

"You didn't tell them, did you? Of course not. All Khmers are afraid of dogs. Dogs are mean, dirty, and they carry nasty diseases. That's why we always carry rocks in our pockets, or at least a stick."

Brian raises his eyebrows and looks at Ash. She shrugs.

"We'll talk about that. Let's finish the introductions."

The last man steps forward.

"I'm Arun. I lost my leg to a mine when I was fourteen while foraging for mushrooms in the jungle. But I was lucky. I got a prosthesis, so I can walk without crutches, and I can work. I can't wait to clear our land so that my kids can play safely."

"Wow. It looks like everyone's life was affected by mines," Brian says.

Vithu nods.

"Of course. Cambodia has more land mines than any other place on earth. That's why we also have the most amputees and countless orphans. Here, nobody is safe from mines. People working their land, kids playing outside, animals grazing, even elephants in the jungle. Our next step may be our last.

Brian sighs.

"Let's get to work then."

**12**

———

Who knew teaching humans to find bombs was so hard? But it was. We, K-9s, could have trained them to sniff those bombs themselves for all the good it did them.

Brian and Ash stretched ropes between trees. We sniffed along with them, then sat and pointed when we smelled explosives. It was just like Mike had taught me, other than the heat, the many new smells, and the creepy-crawlies hiding in the grass. I could do it with my eyes closed and a paw tied behind my back.

The humans made it hard. They didn't like bombs, but they liked dogs even less. They jumped back whenever we touched them, and their fear stank so bad it almost drowned the odor of explosives.

"Keep your hands soft on that lead, Arun. For God's sake, it's not a shovel! It's a freaking leash, and there's a dog attached to it. Let him pull you along, don't hold him up," Brian said.

Arun tried, but, between his metal leg and his fear, he kept jerking Gogol back.

Gogol growled.

"What the heck? Why do I have to fight him for every step? What's so hard about walking along that rope, eh?"

Further left, Vithu did his best to follow Greta without holding her back while keeping as far from her as he could. When they finally made it to the end, Vithu lifted his arm to drop the Kong he held under his arm to reward her without touching her.

Bo, behind me, raked of fear. Her hands shook, but she followed without holding me back. She kept as far from me as she could, and I was glad. I wanted no dog eaters near me.

Chan struggled the most. She shook with fear and jumped back whenever Frieda even glanced at her. That drove Brian nuts.

"Come on, Chan, stay on that rope, will you, girl? Move with the dog; just tag along gently. No! Don't jump back like that! You're pulling that dog away from her job. And what if you step on a mine?"

But Chan feared Frieda more than she feared mines.

By the time the sun got halfway through the sky, we were all exhausted. The air was so thick with steam and strange smells we could hardly breathe, so we all panted with our tongues hanging to our knees.

Ash wiped the sweat off her face.

"Let's take a break. We all need it."

She poured water into our bowls and handed the humans cold drinks.

"See you back here in an hour."

She sat next to Brian in our shelter while the Khmers lay under a banyan tree.

"What do you think?"

"It's harder than I expected. And it's not even about the explosives; it's all about the dogs. I didn't know the Khmers hate dogs. The Bosnians couldn't wait to play with them. I had to keep telling them that the K-9s weren't pets and hold them back; otherwise, they'd have spoiled them rotten. But these four? They'd rather step on a mine than touch the dogs. They don't like them and don't trust them, and the dogs know it. You can't build a team without trust."

Ash nodded.

"True. But the dogs did OK. Even Rambo worked like a champ."

"They won't do it for long. Dogs work with people. If these folks don't get it together, the dogs will lose their training, and we'll have nothing left to work with."

"They need time. These folks have never seen dogs like this. The Khmers only know the packs of street dogs scavenging for food, always ready to attack them. No wonder they're wary. We'll just have to show them that these dogs are different."

"But how? The K-9s picked up on their loathing, and they'll respond in kind. You can only reap what you sow."

"How about we show them how it's done? We take turns working with the dogs while they watch?"

Brian shrugged.

"That's not what I signed up for. I was hoping to sit in the shade with a cold beer and yell at them, telling them how it's done. I didn't come here to sweat my heart out while they watch."

"You have a better plan?"

"No."

**13**

———

Clearing the minefield with Ash was a breeze. I sat to point out the explosives, and she dropped my Kong. I caught it and brought it back. She gave it a few tugs, then scratched my ears and hugged me.

The Kong was great, the praise and the petting were OK, but the hugging felt weird. Mike never did that, and that was fine with me. I like my space, and she was getting a little too personal. Not like she smelled foul or anything, but still. I guess she was just trying to show the Khmers that I was safe and trustworthy, not a mangy rabid stray. Or food.

But old habits die hard. It took like forever until Bo and the others got used to working with us. And if that was hard, teaching them to look after us was even harder. They didn't want to get anywhere near us, let alone touch us.

"You need to check the dogs thoroughly every day," Brian said. "Their backs, heads, and bellies, but also their tails, and all the paws."

Chan blanched with fear, but Brian didn't care.

"You need to check that dog every day. Make sure he has no wounds to fester or ticks or parasites to make him sick. This humid heat will do a number on their paws, and the jungle crawls with critters that bite them and burrow in their skin. And if they get sick, there's no more dogs, no more mine clearing, and no more job. Get it?"

Chan lifted my paw with shaky hands and dropped it like it was hot. Brian shook his head.

"No, no, no! Not like that. Check every footpad and the spaces between his toes. And if you find a wound, you must clean and dress it."

It took forever until the four of them got comfortable enough to work with us. Still, the day came when we all got into the truck and drove to the minefields.

I couldn't wait to see them. We'd been in that camp forever, and I looked forward to seeing something new, so I danced on my paws the whole way.

Frieda growled.

"Take it easy, kid. It's bad enough we have to deal with these rookie handlers. You can't afford to make mistakes. Plus, the minefields are just like our camp. That's why they set it up the way they did."

As always, she was right. The minefields were just like the camp: grasses, bamboo, and a few old banyan trees throwing shade. It was all the same other than the red signs.

"It says, 'Keep Out. Minefield,'" Frieda said.

"Wow! You can read too?"

She wagged her tail in a dog smile.

"That's just about the one thing I can't do. But I recognize the skull and crossbones since I've seen them before."

Ash and Brian stretched ropes between trees, and we started sniffing along them, pulling our handlers along. It was no different from training, but knowing it was real made it exciting.

The Khmers must have felt the same because for the first time ever, they acted like our partners and worked with us to find the mines instead of being wary.

I was sniffing under the twisted roots of an old Banyan tree when the sharp TNT odor hit my nose. I sat and pointed at it. Bo opened her arm to drop the Kong and called.

"Rambo found something."

"Mark it," Brian said.

Bo marked it with a couple of sticks, then they dug out a dirty green plate barely larger than my paw.

Brian brushed the dirt off to see it better.

"It's an antipersonnel mine. It may look small, but it's strong enough to blow off your legs. It could even kill you if you happen to be a kid. It's plastic, made in China, with very little metal, so a metal detector would have trouble finding it. Good job, Bo. You just saved someone's life. Or at least their legs."

Bo's face lit up. She tugged on my Kong and smiled.

"Good job, Rambo."

**14**

———

It didn't take us long to get good at it. How could we not? From dawn to dusk, we did nothing else — but for a midday nap to avoid the worst heat.

But clearing minefields was slow work. We sniffed every inch of every field again and again before calling it clear. It took days and days to get through it, though there were four of us, plus our handlers. Sometimes it felt like it would take forever.

But it wasn't all bad. After seeing us work, the Khmers started treating us with new respect. Vithu and Arun often praised us, and Bo enjoyed tugging on our Kongs. All but Chan, who still smelled like fear.

But the others had fun. They laughed and chatted in a language that sounded like water birds calling. Brian and Ash didn't understand it. We K-9s didn't get the words either, but we didn't need to. We heard the tone, smelled their mood, and listened to their heartbeats, so we got what mattered. We didn't speak English either, but that didn't stop us from understanding Ash and Brian. When we smelled their feelings and read their thoughts, how could we not?

The locals started coming by to watch us work. Some came back every day and stayed for hours: the old woman with black teeth who constantly chewed on betel leaves; the wiry old man with cloudy eyes; the one-legged man leaning on his homemade crutches; the kids with round eyes peeping from behind their mother's sarongs.

Brian didn't like it.

"What are they coming here for?"

The Khmers laughed like they always did when they felt embarrassed. Laughing was their way of saving face.

"This is their land, and they can't wait to have it cleared so they can use it," Vithu said.

"I wish they didn't come. Or at least not so close. What if something happens? What if one of those kids steps on a mine?"

"They know better. And they won't come any closer. They're afraid of the dogs."

But they came back, and they got closer. One day, the old woman shouted something that made Vithu frown. But Bo answered, and they all laughed.

"What did she say?" Ash asked.

"She said we should use metal detectors, like everyone else. Why waste time with the dogs? They'd be better in soup, she said."

Ash's face caught fire, but her voice stayed soft.

"What did you tell her, Bo?"

"I told her to worry about the betel leaves that stole her mind and leave the dogs alone."

Vithu laughed. "She also told her to come and get herself a dog to cook it if she's that hungry."

Ash sighed.

"You guys know why we're using dogs instead of metal detectors, don't you?"

The Khmers shook their heads.

"I'm sorry; I thought we talked about that. Dogs are twenty times faster than metal detectors. Better, too, because metal detectors can only find metal. That might be a mine, but more often than not, it's just shrapnel, lost coins, broken tools, or some other metal scrap, and you'll find hundreds of those for every mine. That slows you down. Plus, metal detectors aren't great at finding plastic mines. But the K-9s sniff explosives, not metal, so they don't waste time on useless scrap. That's why a dog can clear in just one day as much land as a metal detector clears in a month."

"And they're good for soup too," Arun said, but nobody laughed.

The people kept coming and got closer every day.

I was taking my nap in the shade when I smelled something and opened my eyes. A little girl in a blue Dora t-shirt stared at me.

She turned to run away when she saw me move, but I wagged my tail, and she came back.

"Chee."

I pricked my ears.

"Chee. Chee?"

She offered me something that smelled like fish sauce and garlic. I sniffed it, then picked it up. It was salty, chewy, and crunchy, though not easy to get down. I looked for more, but she'd run back to her mom.

"How was it?" Greta asked.

"Spicy and crunchy. Not bad, but for the legs. They got stuck in my throat."

"The legs? What legs? What was it?"

Frieda licked her chops.

"A fried cricket. They're way better than raw."

**15**

———

Wow! Cricket? Really?

Sure, I eat flies when I can catch them — not often — but they're too small to taste like anything but victory. Same with fleas, except they're crunchier. I tried a worm once. It was Dog-awful slobbery, and it tasted like dirt. Bugs are crunchy, but they don't taste like much. But none of these compares to that cricket!

"Why do fried crickets taste so good?"

"Because humans doctor them to give them flavor. Their sense of smell is so poor they can't taste their food unless they add stuff to it. Otherwise, they couldn't tell a cricket from a duck. And everything tastes better fried," Frieda said.

She was right. Everything tastes better fried. That's why we all looked forward to our handlers' gifts.

Gone were the days they didn't want to even touch us. Now, they brought us food — fried crickets, bamboo worms, even chicken bones. Not as a reward for our work — that's what Kongs were for. Just to show appreciation.

Brian didn't like it.

"You can't give people food to dogs. They're on a diet, and they shouldn't get anything else, or they'll get spoiled. Even worse, they'll get sick. Chicken bones are terrible for dogs. They poke holes in their stomachs and kill them."

The Khmers looked at him as if he were nuts, but they stopped giving us treats when he was there. They waited until he looked the other way. But he knew it anyhow.

"Only weeks ago, they wouldn't even touch those dogs, and now they spoil them? That's ridiculous!"

Ash shrugged. "Let them be. Aren't you glad they finally got to love the dogs?"

"They can love them without ruining them."

"But for them, food is love. They feed the dogs to thank them for giving their families a better life. Ever since they started working on this project, their kids haven't gone hungry, and they can even buy them clothes and send them to school. Of course, they're grateful."

"They can be grateful without spoiling my dogs."

"They're not your dogs, Brian."

"So what? While they're in my care, they're my responsibility."

Ash let him be. The Khmers did too. We'd all learned to avoid Brian, even Bo's kids when they visited. Life was better if you stayed away from Brian.

That's why, when Da, Bo's little girl, came to visit, she veered behind the bushes to avoid him. But behind the bushes meant behind the red signs warning you off the minefields.

Da was just three and couldn't read, of course. Still, the red signs should have kept her away. Nobody, not even us dogs, ever ventured there.

We froze when we saw her playing deep in the minefields. Her spiky ponytail fluttered over her blue Dora t-shirt as she plowed the minefield with her wood-carved bull.

Bo screamed. She dropped Freida's leash and took off, but Ash grabbed her arm.

"No!"

Bo shook her off, but Ash wouldn't let go.

"You can't do that, Bo! If you step on a mine, who will look after her?"

Bo's face turned gray.

"What do I do?"

"Tell her to stay there. Don't let her move."

Da heard them talk and waved at Bo.

"Don't move," Ash shouted.

Da took a step. The humans gasped. Bo raised her hands.

"Chop! Stop."

Da took another step.

"Da, chop!"

Da stopped.

"Hitovy? Why?"

Brian's ears turned red.

"Now what? Like I didn't have enough to do! I needed this like a hole in the head."

"Brian, did it ever cross your mind that not everything is about you?" Ash asked.

Brian choked. Ash turned to Bo.

"Listen, Bo. You keep her there. Don't let her move, no matter what. I'll get her back."

Brian groaned.

"No, you won't. This isn't your problem. You didn't send that kid there, and I won't risk having you hurt. You have a job to do, remember? You're here to train the Khmers to clear the minefields, not go on some cockamamie mission and get yourself blown up. And why? To salvage some silly kid that shouldn't have been there in the first place!"

Ash ignored him. She looked from Greta to Gogol, then Frieda and me.

"Rambo? Let's go get Da."

Ash and I had walked through the minefields to look for mines a hundred times. But never like this.

First, there were no ropes. And second, this time we weren't looking for mines. We were looking to avoid them.

Ash clipped her lead to my collar, and I started sniffing my way toward Da, inch by inch. Step after step, I crept closer. Ash followed, stepping in my tracks.

We were past halfway when I got the first whiff of explosive. The wind filled my left ear, and for a moment, I could hear Cersei: Don't let the bombs sniff you first." I veered right and waited.

Nothing happened.

I glanced back.

The humans behind us stood by the ropes like statues. I could tell by their frozen faces that they expected us to blow into smithereens. All but Bo.

She didn't look at us. Her eyes were only on Da. She comforted her, praised her, and talked her into staying put, even though her voice was breaking.

The K-9s were having a blast. Greta and Gogol danced on their feet, wagging their tails.

"Come on, Ram. Show them how it's done," Gogol barked.

"You can do it, kid. Make us proud," Greta answered.

Frieda lay with her nose on her paws. My eyes met hers, and she growled.

"What the heck takes you so long?"

I turned to Da. Ten more steps to the little mound she squatted on, holding her toy to her chest.

Three more.

She reached her arms toward me. I wagged my tail and stepped aside, letting Ash pick her up.

We headed back.

I sniffed every rock, every root, and every inch of dirt like I hadn't just done it. The humans' eyes never left us, and their fear weighed my every step. I could hear their hearts beating like drums. They held their breaths.

It felt like forever until we reached the ropes. Ash gave Da to Bo, who started crying. Ash sighed with relief.

She looked for my Kong, but she'd forgotten it. So she kneeled and hugged me, rubbed my ears, and held me close to her heart.

"Good job, Rambo. What a good job you did! What a good boy you are."

For the first time ever, her hug felt like home.

"Good work, Ash and Rambo. Well done, you two," Brian said, throwing me the Kong and giving it a tug.

"Thanks, Brian."

"Of course. Tell me, Ash, why Rambo? He's the youngest and least experienced. He'd be the last one I'd choose."

Ash shrugged. "I knew I could trust him."

"But you could trust the others too. They're all excellent, well-trained K-9s. Why Rambo?"

Ash sighed. "I don't know. Maybe because he understands."

"Understands what?"

"Me."

## 16

Unlike Brian, who'd rather have a beer with the boys than spend time with us, and the Khmers, who couldn't wait to go home to their families, Ash cared about us. Something in her touch told me she had my back. We completed each other. She had knowledge; I had my nose. She brought her wisdom; I brought my curiosity. She was patient; I was enthusiastic. As a team, we were more than the sum of us apart.

I learned to trust and love my K-9 friends. Greta and Gogol were lots of fun, and Frieda had a story for every occasion: the Malinois who went to take a mud bath and got eaten by the Congo crocodiles; the German shepherd who took off after a cat and lost his leg in Angola; the hungry chocolate Lab who ate poisoned bait in Mozambique. Frieda's stories were never dull, and they made you think twice before making rash decisions, such as squeezing through the open gate.

But I didn't remember any open-door stories that night.

It was late, and my partners were snoozing already. I'd gone to bed too, but my belly got rumbling and wouldn't stop. It must have been that fried tarantula Bo brought. It wasn't that big if you ignored the legs — they're nothing but crunch anyhow — but it packed loads of flavor. Chewy too, so I ate it all, even the eight eyes, the hairy legs, and the spinnerets. Those are the silk glands, Frieda said, whatever silk is. But now it wanted out.

I crawled out of my crate like a shadow since I didn't want the others making fun of me for eating things I knew I shouldn't. I looked for the perfect spot under the palm trees, spun around 720 degrees until I found true north, and dropped it out.

Much better! I lapped some water and crawled back into my crate, and I was about to fall asleep when I heard something squeak.

My ears perked up. That sounded just like the compound's rusty gate, but that's always locked at night. So I went to check. Sure enough, it was open.

Vithu was supposed to lock us up at night. But he hadn't.

A gust of wind pushed the gate open, and I stuck my nose out to take a peek. I couldn't help being curious. We only left the compound when the truck took us to the minefields, but the smells and the sounds from the jungle village traveled over our fence. And I always wondered about the tiny houses covered with banana leaves that smelled like fish sauce and smoke, the long-tailed monkeys playing in the trees, and the packs of local dogs I sometimes saw from the truck.

The gate opened again.

Oh, well. I wasn't doing anything better, and I couldn't resist. I squeezed out the gate toward adventure.

Just stepping out of the compound got me dizzy with excitement. I'd never, ever, been somewhere on my own. The humans always decided where I went, whether it was Brian driving us to the minefields, Mike taking me for a walk, or Hendrik delivering me to the airport. I'd never been on my own, so this new freedom felt exhilarating.

I sniffed my way down dark narrow paths, around tiny houses with golden windows glowing from flickering oil lamps. I soaked my paws in the thick, rich mud of the rice fields that smelled like green stalks and manure.

The scent was so good it made me dizzy, and I couldn't resist. I rolled in the mud, crushing the green stalks until its moist embrace coated me all over. Then I got up, shook, and pushed on.

The fried fish aroma caught my nose. I followed it to a tiny wooden stand, empty now. But I found a fish head in the ditch.

I love fish heads even uncooked, especially after they sit in the sun for a day or two, but stuffed with lemongrass and salt-roasted? Now you're talking!

I dispatched it in two bites, then sniffed for more. No luck.

Oh well. I turned around to go when someone growled.

Not one, not two, but three local dogs had cut off my retreat. Their burning yellow eyes were glued to me, their gleaming fangs and their raised hackles made it clear they weren't looking for a friend.

A large red male sporting an ugly scar stepped forward.

"Barang Dog, what are you doing here? You thought you'd come to check the cuisine?"

My eyes darted left and right, searching for a way out, but there was none.

"I was just passing by."

I glanced back. The thatch-roofed house behind me was taller than I could ever hope to scale. Scarface stood ahead, cutting my way. A shifty-eyed female in a striped coat laughed like a hyena to my left. A long-nosed hound smiled a predatory smile to my right.

I was trapped.

Scarface stepped forward.

"You fat Barang pig! You thought you'd just come over to steal our food, didn't you? Don't your humans feed you?"

I stepped back, trying to act cool.

"I'm sorry, guys. It's just a misunderstanding. I didn't know the fish head was yours. I thought someone threw it away. I'm so sorry."

"You're sorry? Well, you'll be even sorrier when we're done with you...."

A strip of drool dripped down from his muzzle. I focused on it until it hit the ground, since I didn't want to think about how I'd look when they were done with me. I'd never been in a dog fight other than the puppy skirmishes with Arco and Rebel, but I could tell it wouldn't be pretty. My tail tucked between my legs.

"He's scared," Hyena laughed.

Scarface growled.

"Of course, he is. He'd be a fool if he wasn't."

They stepped forward. I stepped back.

I never thought much about fighting. I always thought civilized dogs could find civilized ways to settle disputes. But I could see there was no way to talk these three starving mutts into letting me go. They shivered with excitement and smelled like they couldn't wait to taste my blood.

Dang! How I wished I'd crawled back in my crate instead of squeezing out that gate. If only I'd gone back after my mud bath! If only I'd never smelled that fish head!

But it was too late. Before long, Frieda will get to tell the story of the Dutch shepherd who left his compound to explore the jungle and got eaten by the wild Khmer dogs. Sadly, I won't be there to hear it.

Hyena stepped forward. Long-Nose smiled.

I stepped back and hit the wall.

Darn.

It's now or never, I thought. I smiled my best smile, and I barked my most persuasive speech.

"Come on, guys, what's the point? Surely, we can talk like a pack of civilized animals? I'm sorry about the fish head, but it wasn't that great. It sat in the mud long enough to lose all its crunch. And it was terribly salty. That's really bad for you, you know."

They growled and stepped forward, so close that their hot, stinky breaths hit my face.

Scarface's stomach gurgled. Hyena drooled. Long-Nose licked his lips.

I wished I'd been a better dog.

There was no talking my way out of this one. I took in a deep breath and waited for Scarface to step forward.

He took one stiff step.

I planted my rear paws on the wall and flew over Scarface like a seagull over a fishing boat. By the time he'd turned around, I ran like the wind.

Thank Dog, I thought, running as if my life depended on it. Because it did. I'd left them behind just heartbeats later, but I kept running until I could barely hear them bark their disappointment.

Looking good. I slowed down to sniff my way back to the compound. I caught a whiff of Greta. There, to my right.

I swerved right and picked up the pace. The wind filled my nose with the smell of home, and I could almost feel the compound grass under my paws when the earth opened to swallow me.

**17**

———

I tumbled headfirst into a deep, dark hole. A mind-numbing pain split my leg, and I yelped, but my mouth filled with water. A big splash and I hit the ground. I was drowning in a foot of muddy water, so I struggled to stand, but my leg exploded with pain.

I looked up. Far above, the moon silhouetted my attackers. They'd caught up with me. All they had to do was jump in and get me.

But they didn't. They just circled up above, again and again.

I'd fallen into a pit with steep, muddy walls. Black water to my shoulders covered its narrow bottom, and three pointed sticks stuck out around me, pointing their sharp ends to the sky. The tarp that had covered the pit had caved under my weight, so I'd fallen in and impaled my leg.

I was trapped.

Even if I could scale those steep walls without falling back on the sticks, the Khmer dogs waited for me. They'd rip me to shreds.

They circled the pit, again and again, drooling like crazy. I sort of hoped they'd jump in. In a one-on-one fight, I had a chance. But no way could I fight three.

"Now what?" Long-Nose barked.

Scarface took his time to nibble thoughtfully at a flea on his shoulder before growling.

"We'll have to get him out of there."

Hyena cocked her head.

"Get him out? But why?"

"It's either that or give up. You saw what happened to Barang. If we jump in, we'll get impaled. Plus, there's a dog there, in case you didn't notice. He may be wounded, but his teeth are just fine. And if we get in there, we can't get out. They built these traps right."

"Who did?" Long-Nose asked.

"The Khmer Rouge. Or the Vietnamese. Who knows? To slow down their enemies, they needed them trapped but not killed. Their friends had to stop and get them out. And they rubbed poison on the Punji sticks to get them sick and slow them down."

Hyena stared at him in wonder.

"How do you know all this?"

"My mother told me. Two of my brothers chased a chicken and fell into one of these. They never came out."

"What happened to them?"

"The farmer sold them for dog meat. Humans love dog meat. They even serve it at weddings."

I shivered.

"You think they'll sell that one as dog meat too?"

"Of course. Or they'll keep him for themselves. Unless we manage to get him out. I wouldn't mind a juicy piece."

A shiny strip of drool stretched down from his lips. Scarface licked it off.

"There's got to be something we can throw in that he can climb on. A box? A board? A bucket?"

"But why would he? He knows we're here, waiting."

"Unless he's stupid, he'll take his chances with us rather than sit in that hole waiting for the dawn. That's when farmers come to look for their catch. I don't think he can outrun us again, but that's his best bet."

They went scurrying around, and I checked the walls. Scarface was right; I'd rather take my chance with them than turn into dog meat.

The six-foot walls were steep and crumbly. On a good day, I could scale a six-foot fence from a running start. But this wasn't a good day; my hind leg was torn, and I had no room to gain momentum. And that freaking crumbly dirt wouldn't let me claw my way up like a solid wood fence.

I couldn't make it out. Not on my own.

So I waited. And planned.

If I managed to get out, I'd go for Scarface first. He's bigger, stronger, and brighter than the others. The other two might run away if I managed to beat him. But how the heck would I beat him? Scarface looked like he lived to fight, while I'd never fought before.

I wasn't done thinking when something hit my head. It was one of those boxes holding plastic bottles, just tall enough to let me reach the edge of the pit. Climbing out on it would have been a breeze but for my painful leg, the crumbly walls, and those three hungry mongrels.

I looked up. Three pairs of burning eyes watched me.

I didn't move.

"Come on, fat boy. What are you waiting for? The dog-meat truck? You're dog meat either way. But, with us, you stand a chance. With them, you don't. You know why? Because they won't take you out alive. They'll drown you right there in that muck. That's what that water is for. They'll bring more. And if you think you can outsmart them and swim, think again. All dogs can swim. That's why they'll first drop this iron grate on you. To keep you on the bottom."

My stomach turned. I wanted to puke, but I yawned instead.

I watched them watch me.

"Come on, Barang. Come up and fight like a dog; don't sit there to die like a sheep. Are all Barangs cowards like you?"

I waited. I didn't know what I was waiting for, but I knew that I had to pick the right moment to have a fighting chance.

I waited. They waited.

Suddenly, Scarface's ears perked up. He jumped to his feet and turned to sniff the air. The others did too.

My time has come. I ignore the pain and climb on the box. It's awfully narrow for my four paws, but then so were the hydrants I climbed in my training. I plant my hind legs, then leap to grab onto the edge of the pit with my front paws. I claw my way up with my back legs — one, two, three — just as Scarface turns to face me.

His yellow fangs gleam, and his pupils grow into black holes as he jumps at my throat. He thinks I'll leap to grab him, but I don't. I twist instead, and I feel his teeth graze my shoulder. I lean into him with all my weight, then watch the pit walls crumble to swallow him.

He screams. The water splashes.

I wonder if he impaled himself too, but I don't get to check. Hyena is closing in on me, foaming at the mouth. I step back. Long-Nose steps forward, growling like a bad muffler.

With Scarface's pit right behind me, Hyena cutting off my left, and Long-Nose closing my right, there's no place to run.

Like it or not, it's time to fight. I turn right to Long-Nose, but Hyena leaps forward, her eyes burning with hate.

I turn to face her, and Long-Nose's stinky breath hits my nostrils.

This looks like the end. I wish I was a better dog.

"Back, you filthy mongrels."

Frieda's growl is music to my ears. Her teeth bared, her hackles up, she's a fury about to tear Long-Nose apart.

Hyena leaps at her throat.

"Don't even think about it," Greta barks.

"I always wondered how dog meat tastes, and it looks like I'm about to find out," Gogol says.

But he didn't. Before you could bark "Milk-Bone," Hyena and Long-Nose had vanished like they'd never been there.

The sun drips blood on our camp as I limp back in.

Somewhere far behind, Scarface screams.

"I wish we could let him out."

Freida yawns.

"He won't be there long."

**18**

———————

"What the heck!?"

Brian shrieked so loud that the two ugly birds quibbling over a worm in the banyan tree stopped to stare at him with curious eyes.

He put his hands on his hips and watched us file in through the gate: First Frieda, then me, then Greta, followed by Gogol, all with our tails between our legs. We all looked guilty, even though the others did nothing but get me out of trouble.

Brian glared at us, then turned to Vithu.

"Did you lock that gate last night?"

Vithu shrank. If he had a tail, he'd have tucked it between his legs, like us. But he didn't, so he did what humans do to get out of trouble: he lied.

"I locked the gate. I swear I did. I remember checking it last night. I don't know how they got out."

Brian's mouth zipped into a line.

"Was that gate open when you came in this morning? Yes or no?"

"Yes...no...I can't remember."

The stench of Vithu's guilt fouled the air. We all knew he was lying, even Brian, but he didn't get to question him any further because Bo and Ash walked in.

"Ash, the dogs just came back from God knows where. They somehow managed to escape last night, and I don't know where they've been. Let's check them out to make sure they're OK."

Brian grabbed Gogol while Ash checked Frieda. The old girl yelped when Ash found the spot where Hyena had bitten her.

"Her shoulder hurts, but I can't see anything."

"Check the others, then," Brian said. Ash rubbed Frieda's ears and let her go. She reached for me, but I yelped as soon as she touched me where Scarface's teeth had dug in.

"Rambo's hurt too."

Her hands were gentle as she checked me all over, but by then, everything hurt. The bite on my shoulder, the gash in my hip, even the paws I'd skinned when I clawed my way out the pit — everything hurt. I was a mass of shivering pain.

Ash shook her head.

"Rambo is sick. We need to take him to the vet."

Brian mumbled something under his breath, something about useless Khmer handlers and stupid dogs, then glanced at me and sighed.

"Ash, you go. Take Bo with you to translate. There's no point in us both wasting our time. I'll take care of things here."

I don't remember the trip, but I remember the vet, a slight man with narrow eyes. He touched my nose and frowned, then opened my mouth to check my gums and stuck some tubes in his ears to listen to my chest. He took them off and shook his head.

"What happened to this dog?"

"Rambo is one of our mine-sniffing dogs. They all took off last night and came back this morning. The others looked OK, but Rambo looked sick."

The vet nodded.

"See this gash on his leg? It's red and hot. It's infected already, so I can't stitch it, or I'll lock the infection inside. The shoulder wound looks like a dog bite. He must have gotten into a fight. For his sake, I hope he fought your other dogs."

Ash shook her head.

"No way. These dogs have been together for months, and they've never had a problem. Never. And the other dogs look fine. But for Frieda. But she's like his mom. I'm sure it wasn't one of them."

The vet shrugged.

"That makes it even worse. If this dog got bit by a street dog, he's in trouble. These dogs are rarely vaccinated, and rabies is endemic here, and it's always lethal. We don't even know which dog he fought with to check him. That's bad news. Even if your dog looked great, we'd still have to put him in isolation and watch him for weeks. But he doesn't. He looks terrible. I think the best thing would be to put him down."

Bo's eyes filled with tears.

"What's he saying?" Ash asked.

"He wants to put Rambo down. He's worried about rabies."

"Nonsense. Rambo is vaccinated every which way; no way can he catch rabies."

Bo translated. The vet shrugged.

"Actually, he can. No vaccine is 100 percent effective, and there are documented cases of vaccinated dogs getting rabies. He absolutely must be isolated, and that will cost a lot of money for a dog that's unlikely to make it. Just look at him. See him shiver? Don't you want to stop his suffering?"

A chill shook me like a tree in November. I shivered so bad I almost bit my tongue, then my eyes went fuzzy like I swam underwater. My brain too. I shook my head to clear it, but it didn't help.

Ash shook her head.

"Absolutely not. We'll do whatever it takes to take care of Rambo. I don't care how much it costs. What do you need to do?"

"I'll clean his wounds and give him a rabies booster. I'll isolate him, of course, and start him on parenteral antibiotics. But it's a long shot. I think he's septic already, and I know very few things that get septic so fast. If I had to guess, I'd say he fell into one of the pits the locals trap dogs in. They sharpen the Punji sticks and season them with every kind of badness, from feces to poison. That would explain why he got so sick so fast. Your dog is in trouble."

"Do whatever you need to do and give him whatever he needs. I'll pay."

The vet shrugged.

"It won't be cheap. And it may not work. If it was my dog..."

Bo raised her voice for the first time ever.

"But he's not your dog, is he? So, do what she told you. This dog is a hero. He saved my daughter's life. Nothing is too good for him."

The vet cleaned my wounds and then gave me a shot. By the time he picked me up to lock me in a crate, my whole body was on fire, but I still shivered. My vision grayed, then turned black, and my nose dropped on my paws.

I tried to open my eyes, but I couldn't. I smelled lavender, and I felt Ash's hands petting me.

"Don't worry, Rambo. We'll take good care of you."

I tried to lick her hand, but I couldn't find it. And I didn't know what she meant. I wasn't worried; I was just tired. So tired that I couldn't think.

Then the world went off.

**19**

———————

I must have slept like a rock because I woke up somewhere else. I smelled the difference even before I opened my eyes. This air's cold and dry, and it smells like disinfectants and pain instead of Cambodia's humid smell of fish sauce, smoke, and rot.

I open my eyes inside a wire cage. One of many, all full of dogs.

Well, no, not all. There's a nasty cat or two — other than Tyrion, all cats are terrible people, always ready to play tricks on you. And I'll be darned if I don't sniff a ferret? But for the most part, it's dogs — big, small, white, black, or spotted. And they all smell sick.

To my right is a Great Dane as big as a SMART car. He smells friendly enough, even though his casted leg sounds like a drum. You wouldn't want that dude stepping on you.

To my left, a small orange mutt keeps his tail between his legs and can't stop scratching like he's got mange. The one-eared orange cat above me loves taunting him, and he never tires of making fun of the mutt's teary eyes and shy tail. The mutt shivers but says nothing, which drives the German shepherd across from him stark mad. She's almost black, other than the heavy white bandage across her chest and the thick golden eyebrows making her look surprised.

I'm still checking who's who when a woman in dark scrubs clips a leash to my collar and takes me to a small green room to see the vet. I know the man with thick round glasses is a vet even though I've never met him. Maybe because he smells like soap, disinfectant, and treats, just like the one in Cambodia.

The man shines a light in my eyes, listens to my chest, and opens the bandage on my hip to check my wound.

"How are you doing, Rambo?"

"Fine, thanks. You?"

"No, seriously. How do you feel?"

"OK. Where am I?"

"In Texas. The Lakeland Veterinary Hospital. They transferred you from Cambodia. Someone named Ash said you're a bomb-sniffing hero. I don't know what strings she pulled to send you here, but she did it. And, after weeks of being so sick that we thought you would die, it finally looks like you'll make it. Do you remember anything?"

"The vet said I might have rabies and wanted to put me down."

"Well, he didn't, and you don't. He did a good job. You're young and healthy, so you managed to pull through. Look at you!"

I looked at myself, but there wasn't much to see. I was still brindle and short-haired. My leg still hurt where I'd torn it in the pit. And I was tired.

"Just a few more days, and we'll let you go."

"Go where?"

"Good question. I don't know. Wherever you belong, I guess?"

That got me thinking. Where do I belong? I belonged in the Netherlands, but they sent me to the States. But I didn't really belong there either; that's why Mike shipped me to Cambodia. But then they sent me here. Where the heck do I belong?

I was still wondering when the tech took me back to my cage. I fell asleep and dreamed I was back in Cambodia, fighting Long-Nose and Hyena, when Frieda barked so loud she woke me up.

But it wasn't Frieda. The German shepherd with brown

eyebrows flashed her white fangs and barked at the orange cat like he was bringing the mail.

"You miserable Van Gogh, stop taunting that mutt right now, or you'll be sorry."

The cat stared at her with glassy round eyes and hissed.

"You, K-9! How do you know my name?"

"I know everything! I work for the CIA. You'll leave that dog alone, or I'll bark out loud for everyone to hear what you did. You and I both know it, Van Gogh. You just taunt that dog one more time, and I'll let the cat out of the bag. Every one of these dogs will laugh at you. The cats too. Even the ferret."

Van Gogh's pupils dilated with fear. Being the laughingstock of a ferret? I can't imagine worse humiliation. Unless it were a hamster. He hissed once more to save face, then pulled his tail over his nose and curled to sleep. The orange mutt melted with gratitude.

"Thank you, Ma'am. Thank you! I can't tell you how grateful I am."

The German shepherd sighed.

"I'm not Ma'am. I'm K-9 Corporal Guinness van Jones. You?"

The mutt's tail quivered.

"I'm Charlie, Ma'am. Corporal, I mean. Are you with the army?"

"I used to sniff for IEDs in Afghanistan, but I retired. How about you? What do you do?"

Charlie's tail wagged so hard his whole curly butt wiggled with it. I could tell he had a major crush on Guinness, who was twice his size. Brian was right. Size doesn't matter.

"This and that. Would you please tell me about your work? Is it hard to sniff bombs? You must be so brave!"

Guinness wanted no part of his adoration, but there was no getting rid of him. So she told him about some yellow lab named Butter, who had lost a leg sniffing IEDs.

"She wasn't purebred, but she was the kindest, nicest, and the most heroic dog I ever met."

Charlie's eyes watered. He scratched his right ear, then the left, and started nibbling on his shoulder like he had fleas. But he was just emoting.

"What a wonderful story!"

"How about you, Charlie? What do you do? Where do you live?"

Charlie wilted.

"Here and there. I'm... I'm not a purebred, you know. I'm just a mutt."

Guinness jumped to her paws and barked.

"What are you talking about? You're not just a mutt. You're a Dog, and there's no higher calling. We're here to guide and protect our humans, who are so thick and clumsy they couldn't make it through life on their own. Your breed, your size, your color — none of that matters. The only thing that matters is your soul."

Charlie's ears flattened. He stepped back.

"Yes, ma'am. Corporal, I mean."

"So, what do you do?"

"I... I used to live in the streets. I spent a lot of time looking for food. And avoiding cars — they're as bad as cats, you know. And merciless. They don't even need to be angry to kill you."

"You're saying you were a free dog?"

Charlie's ears went up.

"I guess you could say that."

"What a hard life! But awesome! I always wondered how it felt."

"Not so good, to be honest. I mostly struggled to stay alive."

"And then?"

"I found a family. The man was an old veteran, and his wife was kind. They fed me, and I started trusting them. I let them come close. But then they caught me and brought me here."

"Why?"

"I thought it was because I had mange, and they were trying to help me. But the cat..."

"Forget the cat. They're all terrible people. The best thing you can do is ignore them. Every one of them is better lost than found. So?"

"They didn't return. I'm still waiting, but..."

"There's no 'but.' They'll return, I promise. And that's an order."

"Yes, Corporal."

"Now, tell me about life in the streets. I've been considering it."

"Living in the streets? You?"

"Of course. How is it?"

Charlie yawned.

"Some days are more fun than others. Summers are nice. It's warm, and the kids play outside and drop food. I once got a whole burger. The kid didn't like the toy it came with, so he threw it away. I didn't like the toy either. It smelled like fries but tasted like plastic. But the burger was still warm.

"Winters are rough. It's cold, and there's no food. Nothing but what you find in the garbage. The cats always got the better pieces. The big dogs too. We, small dogs, went hungry more often than not. All in all, I wouldn't recommend it."

"How long did you do this for?"

"The whole summer and fall, and half the winter. Then I found the family who fed me. But then they left me here...."

**20**

———————

I couldn't imagine why an explosive-detecting K-9 would want to live in the streets, so I thought I'd ask.

"Corporal Guinness? My name's Rambo. I work in the same line of business. I just returned from Cambodia."

The brown eyebrows raised.

"Cambodia? Wow! What happened to you? Stepped on a mine?"

My ears flattened. I'll never live this down.

"Not exactly. I got into a...conversation with a pack of local dogs over a fish head, and I got hurt. But I'm interested in your work. How was Afghanistan?"

Guinness yawned. In dog language, a yawn is worth a thousand words, none of them good. We yawn when we're tired, yawn when we're sick, and yawn when we're upset. And sometimes when we're sleepy. But then we seldom bother. We just nap.

"Not as fun as you'd think. Kandahar is hot, dusty, and boring. And when it's not boring, it's deadly. I'd rather hear about Cambodia. Did you like it?"

"I did. It was work, but it wasn't hard. You were good as long as you followed the ropes and sniffed every inch. And..."

"Ropes? What ropes?"

"The ropes the handlers marked the terrain with. That's how we knew what was cleared and what wasn't."

Guinness looked at me like I'd grown a third ear.

"You mean they told you where to sniff?"

"Of course. Didn't your handlers do the same?"

Guinness choked with laughter.

"Of course not. We told them. We knew where we needed to go, so we sniffed a safe path there and back. But nothing was ever safe outside the wire. And there was no such thing as cleared. We had to sniff the path again and again, even if we returned an hour later. You never knew when some joker would plant an IED behind your back."

"Outside the wire?"

"Yes. Our barracks were surrounded by razor wire to keep out the riffraff. Didn't you have the same in Cambodia?"

"No. We lived in an outdoor compound. We only had a rain shelter and..."

"Rain shelter? It rains there?"

"Every day. Sometimes more than once."

Guinness cocked her head.

"Wow! Lucky you! I didn't see a drop of rain throughout my time in Kandahar. No mud, either."

"No mud? Really? That's terrible!"

"Awful. Nothing but that darn orange desert. Tell me, did the locals shoot at you?"

"No."

"Did they throw grenades?"

"Of course not."

"So, how did they try to kill you?"

Good question.

"Well, there was this pit with poisoned, sharp sticks. That's where they drown the dogs they kill for meat. But I got there by mistake. The locals didn't really want to kill us. They were happy to see us clear their land."

"Happy?"

"Yes. We cleared the fields so they could work them, let the bulls graze, and let the kids play outside. They came to watch us every day."

The eyebrows went up.

"You mean they liked having you there?"

"Of course. The kids even brought us fried tarantulas or crickets. They were yummy."

"Wow! Where do you sign up for this? Rain, mud, gifts, and no grenades? You don't know how lucky you are!"

"Really?"

"Kandahar is not like that. There's no rain and no mud. Nothing but endless dusty desert. And the people hate you. They have nothing for you but IEDs, bullets, and grenades. If they ever gave you something, you shouldn't take it. It would either be poisoned or blow up in your face. Everyone hated us there. There was nothing but death and destruction."

Guinness sighed and curled into a ball. She pulled her tail over her eyes, pretending to sleep, and her sour smell of misery filled my nose. My questions brought back bad memories, and I was sorry I asked.

"Why did you do that?" Charlie growled.

I flattened my ears in shame.

"So sorry. I was just comparing notes since we're in the same business. I didn't mean to upset her."

The orange cat chuckled.

"Well done, you ugly brindle mutt!"

Charlie bared his teeth and barked: "Shut up, you stupid feline!"

Van Gogh hissed but shut up.

"Sorry, Guinness. I didn't mean to upset you," I said.

"It's not you. It's my memories. Kandahar is a terrible place. Don't ever go there," she growled.

"I won't."

Little did I know.

## 21

———

Sleep wouldn't come near me that night. Guinness's sadness reminded me of my own. I missed my pack.

Frieda, Greta, Gogol, and I were just partners at first. But the night they broke the rules to rescue me, they became my family.

They surrounded me like bodyguards all the way back from the punji stick pit. Frieda went first, sniffing our way, while Greta and Gogol protected my sides. I was touched, but I felt terrible to cause so much trouble.

"Thanks, guys. I'm OK."

Greta snorted. "You're not OK. Look at you! You're practically crawling!"

She was right, of course. The shoulder Scarface bit didn't feel good, but the real problem was my torn leg. It throbbed with so much pain I couldn't put any weight on it. I couldn't even hold it up by halfway, so I let it drag through the dirt.

"Thank Dog, we're out of danger. Those mutts vanished when they saw you."

Gogol growled. "The heck they did. Look back. See those yellow pairs of eyes? That's them and their friends. They smelled your blood from miles away, and it made them hungry. We'd better get back in the compound before every mutt in the jungle comes looking for dinner. They'll be too many to fight."

I tried to hustle, but the leg wouldn't let me. So I tried to distract them.

"How did you know I was in trouble? And how did you find me?"

Frieda glared. "What do you think?"

"By smell?"

She shook her head like I didn't deserve an answer and pushed on.

A cloud covered the moon, and the night got darker. Something shook the trees, and someone laughed up above. Far away, someone screamed, and someone else answered right behind me. Then something moved under my feet, and my heart skipped a beat.

The strange scents of unknown creatures filled my nose; then I caught a whiff of wild dog coming from behind. I glanced back. Four pairs of yellow eyes followed us.

"How did you know I was in trouble?"

"I saw you leave. I couldn't believe it! I know you're just a pup, but for Dog's sake, even you should have more sense than going out at night in a place you know nothing about! We knew we had to come and get you when we heard you bark."

My tail tucked between my legs.

"Thank you for saving me."

"You spoke too soon. I think they're coming," Greta growled.

I glanced back. A dozen glowing yellow eyes getting closer.

Gogol looked back.

"Frieda, you take him back. Greta and I will keep them here to buy you time."

"But..."

Frieda picked up the pace.

"Shut up and move, kid. Otherwise, those two will die for nothing."

I followed her as fast as I could, wishing I could look back.

"The white one first," Greta growled.

"OK," Gogol barked.

The night exploded into a frenzy of snarling, barking, and growling. The jungle went quiet, listening to the fight.

"To your left," Greta barked. Gogol growled like a chainsaw; then someone yelped. A terrible scream split the night, then another.

I shivered.

"Hurry up," Frieda growled.

Another heart-wrenching scream, then another. The agonal cries started fading, covered by hungry voices I couldn't recognize.

"Come on, pup. Move!"

Just five more steps to the black gate framing the blood-red sky. But I didn't have five steps left in me.

I heard a branch break behind us, then someone's heavy panting. They were close.

But the gate was too far.

Frieda grabbed me by the collar and dragged me in just as Gogol and Greta caught up with us.

Frieda wagged her tail.

"Good job, you two. What happened to the pack?"

"They stopped to look after the white one," Greta said.

Looking smug, Gogol licked a blood drop off his shoulder.

Frieda licked their noses.

"Not bad for a pair of Belgians."

"You too, for a German," Greta said.

I wished I'd gotten to thank them for saving my life, but I didn't get to. Ash took me to the vet, and I don't know what happened next. I hope they didn't get in trouble with Brian, and I wonder how they're doing.

I miss Frieda. She wasn't cuddly, but she always had my back.

She never complained, even when she hurt. I knew it from the curve of her back, the pain in her eyes, and her smell. I hope Ash looks after her and she gets enough rest. Dog knows the old girl deserves it.

I miss hearing Greta and Gogol bicker about something or other like they always did. But they were brave, loyal, and always there if you needed them.

I miss Bo and Da, who always brought me something when she visited — a frog leg, a fried cricket, or at least a leaf. I ate them, even the leaf, just to be polite. I hoped it wasn't poisonous. One day she brought a betel nut, the kind they chew to get high. It was so spicy it made my tongue numb, so I spat it, but she insisted. I ate it, and I got so wired I had to run laps around the compound, but I still couldn't sleep all night.

I miss them all. And I miss Ash.

## 22

That's why I hoped they'd send me back to Cambodia. I couldn't wait to see them all and tell Frieda, Greta, and Gogol to stay away from Kandahar.

But they didn't. When they let me go, Ash wasn't the one waiting for me. Mike was.

I recognized the road, even though it felt like years since I'd been there. The trees were naked, and the grass had burned into brown. A freezing wind chased flocks of dark clouds across a heavy sky, making me wish I was back in Cambodia waiting for the rain. I'd be listening to the monkeys quarrel in the banana trees and hear the elephants scream down the river. I'd sniff the rich mud smelling like fish sauce and rotten bananas; I'd look for crickets and listen to Frieda snore in her crate.

But this wasn't Cambodia.

The white house at the end of the driveway was lonely and silent. Nothing moved but the dark plume of smoke spitting out of the brick chimney.

Mike let me out, and I limped to the bushes to bless them and catch up with the news. But it had just rained, and the scents got washed off. A rabbit, two squirrels. And...

Something jumped me.

"You're back! You're back!"

A humongous smoke-colored cat bit my ear. His green eyes looked into mine, and he purred.

"I missed you!"

Tyrion? But he was only as big as an orange! This thing is bigger than a watermelon and just as heavy.

"Cersei said you wouldn't come back. She said you'd step on some bomb and blow up, but I knew better. I told her you'd return."

He licks my face and rubs himself against me, and I don't know whether to be happy or embarrassed. He's just a cat, for Dog's sake! But it feels good to be wanted. And I missed him too.

I lick his face until his fur sticks up like a mohawk. He may be just a cat, but at least he's happy to see me. I've been so lonely.

"So good to see you, Tyrion. How did you get so big?"

"Of course, he did. That useless cat does nothing but eat and sleep all day," Cersei growls from the door.

She sniffs the air with her long, gray muzzle, and her shaggy orange coat looks too big for her.

The old girl has aged since I left.

I wonder how she feels about my return. She didn't like me last time. So I wag my tail in a cautious hello.

"Hi, Cersei. Good to see you."

She lifts her muzzle to sniff me, but the wind's going the wrong way.

"How are you doing, Cersei?"

She cocks her head.

"Rambo? Is that you?"

"Of course."

She takes two shaky steps and sniffs again.

"It is you! I didn't think I'd see you again!"

Her fluffy tail wags like a flag, but she's not looking at me. Her cloudy white eyes stare at something behind me.

I glance back. There's nothing there.

That's when it dawns on me that she can't see me. She's blind.

I step forward to lick her nose. She licks me back.

"Good to see you, Cersei."

"How're you doing, kid?"

She sniffs my butt.

"You got hurt?"

"Yes."

"A bomb?"

"No. Just being young and foolish. But I'm better now."

"Good."

"How are you doing, Cersei?"

"I'm old. And tired. Take me back inside?"

We climb the three steps shoulder to shoulder, one small step after another. I match my limp to her shuffle to go through the door. The empty house smells like smoke, Mike, and beer.

I glance at the fake-wood floors, the empty dinner table, and the old sofa Cersei used to chase me from. Cersei sniffs her way back up to her old spot. She curls there, then slams her tail in an invite.

"Come sit with me, Rambo."

I jump on the sofa and leave her some space, but she crawls until she touches my shoulder and sighs.

"I'm glad you're back!"

Tyrion curls between my paws.

"Me too. Me too!"

I'm glad to be here, even though Tyrion is just a cat, and Cersei's white eyes break my heart. Few things in life hurt worse than watching a good dog grow old. But they're my pack now, and I'm happy to have them.

"Me three. I'm glad to be back."

**23**

Mike laughed when he found us.

"You made yourself quite at home, didn't you? Good. I can see the old girl's glad to have you back. Take care of her, will you?"

I did. From then on, Cersei and I did everything together. We stepped out every morning at the break of dawn to bless the bushes and check the peemail. Mike fed us breakfast; then we all walked the fences and checked on the cows. We came back to lay on the porch, soaking the sun, until we took off to chase squirrels. We ran shoulder to shoulder, barking at them, but we never caught one.

Tyrion laughed at us.

"That's because you bark like two maniacs. That's not how you catch a squirrel! You must be patient and stealthy. You lay in the shade and watch them get closer and closer until they're close enough to pounce on. And wham!"

Cersei bared her teeth in a smile.

"Listen, cat. My eyes are past watching squirrels or anything else. Rambo and I, we're not into catching squirrels. What's the point? They aren't even cooked. We're talking about chasing them. That's where the fun is."

Tyrion fluffed himself like a toilet brush.

"I beg to differ. For me, the sport starts AFTER I catch them."

A red gleam passed through his eyes, and I was glad I wasn't a squirrel.

Day after day went easy and quiet, with long naps and short walks, just right for Cersei's stiff joints and my healing leg. It was so quiet that I finally noticed that Mike's kids and Linda were missing.

"Where are they?"

Cersei snorted.

"You noticed already? It only took you what? A month?"

"Come on. Where are they?"

"I don't know where they went. Mike and Linda had been struggling for a while. After you left, there was even more yelling. Mike didn't say much, but I think he missed you. Linda wasn't happy either. She kept harping on him about one thing or another. Then one day, she packed the kids in her new car and left. I haven't seen her since, but I can sometimes smell the kids on Mike."

That must have been why Mike always smelled so sad. He and Linda used to fight so much, you'd have thought he'd be happier alone, but he smelled anything but happy. Especially when he went to bed. He took off his legs, leaned them against the wall, then turned off the light and crawled under the covers, leaving the radio on.

Cersei sighed.

"He always does that. That makes him feel like he's not alone."

Tyrion stared at her like she was nuts.

"Of course not. We're here too, remember?"

"We are, but we don't count. We're not humans."

Tyrion hissed.

"Good! Who wants to be human? They're pathetic! Even Mike. He couldn't climb a tree to save his life! As for catching a mouse, forget it! Not if it was the last thing left to eat on earth. And the stupid things he does all day. He stares at fences, counts cows, and watches gibberish on TV! He barely ever naps. How does that make any sense? We're not humans; we're far superior. At least I am!"

Cersei shook her head.

"You stupid cat! Where do you think your food comes from?"

"From a can, thank you. I approve of getting food. And opening cans. But everything else…"

"Mike's the one who feeds you, you ungrateful feline! He keeps a roof above your head and looks after you when you're sick, like when you stole the neighbor's fish, remember? You should be grateful!"

Tyrion's green eyes rounded in wonder.

"Grateful? What's grateful?"

"There's cats for you. Stupid, ungrateful, and useless," Cersei growled.

Days went by. Tyrion and Cersei kept bickering about something or other, Mike did his thing, and my leg healed. I even stopped limping unless I was tired.

Then, one day, Mike invited me into the truck.

"Where are you going?" Cersei asked.

"I don't know."

She sniffed Mike's way, and her hackles went up.

"I don't like this. Be careful, Rambo."

"Of course," I said, but I wondered if she'd started to lose it. What was there to worry about?

We drove to Butch's. I sniffed high and low for Arco, but I got nothing. He'd gone somewhere, and I just hoped it wasn't Kandahar.

Butch checked me out.

"How's he doing?"

"As good as new."

"Fantastic. You have a week to do a refresher. I got him a job."

"Already? You're sending him back to Cambodia?"

"Cambodia? Nope. That's done and paid for. He's going to clear minefields in Angola."

**24**

Angola it was. Then Madagascar. Then Egypt. The one place I didn't want to go was Kandahar.

I had just returned from Egypt when Butch told Mike, "Rambo's going to need some training for his next job."

"Sure, I'll do a refresher."

"No, not a refresher. This is a whole new job. No more mine-clearing; he'll be looking for IEDs."

"You're kidding, right?"

"Not in the least."

"But Rambo isn't an IED sniffer; he's a mine-clearing K-9. That's what he's always done."

"I know, Mike. I sent him there, remember? But you'll have to reprogram him for this one. He's an explosive-detecting K-9. Switching him from IEDs to mines may be a challenge, but switching him from mines to IEDs should be a piece of cake. And you have a month."

"But why?"

"I have no customers for a mine-clearing dog right now, but the US Army needs an explosive-detecting K-9 in Afghanistan. He's going to Kandahar."

My ears perked up. I didn't get most of what Butch said, but I got Kandahar, and I didn't like it.

Neither did Mike.

"Why Rambo? He's already specialized in mine clearing, and he's doing great. How about training one of the new dogs?"

Butch shook his head.

"There's no time. Training a new dog will take much longer than switching Rambo. He's already familiar with most of the explosives and the technique. And the contract is for him. They asked for him by name."

"Why?"

"Who knows? And how does it matter?"

So Mike and I started training again. There were no ropes to follow and no pulling on my leash to lead me, but other than that, it was just the same. I sniffed for explosives, then I sat to point them out to Mike, and he gave me my Kong.

I already knew TNT, plastics, and black powder. I learned to sniff fertilizers, urea nitrate, TATP, HMTD, and other stuff even Mike couldn't spell. He mixed them with bacon, fish, coffee, soap, and garlic to mask the odor, but telling them apart was easy. Fun too, so I looked forward to my training.

Tyrion didn't.

"What do you do that for? None of those smells is worth finding if you ask me. Now, if it was some Albacore tuna, a fried chicken leg, or even salami..."

Cersei growled. "But nobody asked you, did they? And you miss the point. Rambo doesn't sniff for the sake of the smells. He looks for whatever gives the smell, which is a bomb. And what you want to do is stay away from it. I don't like this one bit, Rambo."

I wagged my tail in sympathy, but she was on a roll.

"If you thought sniffing mines was dangerous, think again. IEDs are way worse. Those mines sat there forever, but the IEDs? They plant them to hurt you. And whoever put them there is looking for a way to kill you."

"How do you know that?" Tyrion asked.

Cersei yawned. "Because I'm a dog, not a stupid cat like you. And I saw it on TV, in this movie about Max, the bomb-sniffing dog."

"What happened to him?"

"I don't know. Mike couldn't stand to watch it, so he changed the channel. But I bet it wasn't anything good. Rambo, I don't like this one bit. What if you don't come back?"

I licked her nose, but I was worried too. Leaving her got harder and harder every time. I always wondered if she'd be there when I returned. Every time she got frailer, weaker, and older.

Tyrion wagged his tail in annoyance. Unlike dogs, who wag their tails when they're happy, cats only wag their tails when they're not.

"That's what you said when he went to Cambodia and Egypt. That's what you say every time. But he came back. He'll come back again."

Cersei sighed. "For once, I hope you're right. And I hope I'm still here to see him."

Tyrion opened his mouth to say that she couldn't see me anyhow, so I nudged him in the ribs to keep him quiet.

When I saw Mike put my crate in the truck, I knew it was time.

I said goodbye to Tyrion. He wrapped himself around my legs and purred.

"Come back soon, will you? I'll miss you. And that old hag never stops complaining when you aren't here. She keeps talking about every terrible thing that could happen to you. I wish she kept it to herself."

I licked him into a mohawk.

"I'll be back."

I licked Cersei's nose. "Goodbye, Cersei. Be well. I'll be back."

"You'd better. I'll be waiting."

Mike closed my crate and started the truck.

I looked back.

Tyrion and Cersei stood on the porch, shoulder to shoulder. Tyrion's tail beat a mile a minute, and Cersei's white eyes watched the sound of the truck taking me away.

I watched them grow smaller until they were all gone, then I curled in my crate with a heavy heart.

"Don't go to Kandahar," Guinness had said.

I wished I could have listened.

**25**

———

That trip took forever.

I curled in my crate with my nose on my paws, listening to the humming of the engines, and thought about Kandahar. Guinness said it was nothing like Cambodia. Was it like Egypt, I wondered? That desert was hot and dry and had more sand than anyone could ever want. But they didn't try to shoot me, and I didn't have to duck grenades. Kandahar must be worse. That sounded so terrible I didn't want to think about it. So, to take my mind off it, I thought of Mike, Tyrion, and Cersei.

How will Cersei manage alone? Her eyes are gone, and her hips are giving up too. Just yesterday, she had trouble going down the porch steps. And it took her forever to get back.

Will Tyrion help her? Probably not. And Cersei wouldn't want his help anyhow. For some reason, those two get along like cats and dogs.

That made me so sad I fell asleep. Then I woke up and fell asleep again. By the time the plane finally landed and I smelled the desert dust, I felt like I'd been locked in that crate forever.

They loaded me on a cart, then dropped me with a pile of luggage.

I waited.

The place smelled like dust, smoke, and anger. I kept sniffing, hoping someone would come to let me out, but nobody did.

I waited and waited until I fell asleep again, and I dreamed I was back in Cambodia with Ash. I woke up to the sound of steps coming toward me.

I sniffed.

That can't be.

I sniffed again.

"Rambo? Is that you?"

She kneeled by my crate. I saw her worried eyes and smelled the lavender on her hands, but I still couldn't believe it.

"Ash? Is that you?"

"Oh, Rambo, I'm so glad to see you! I thought I'd never see you again!"

"Same here. How did you get here?"

She shook her head. Her fine blonde hair floated around her, then settled back. "It's a long story. I'll tell you. But first, how have you been?"

"Not bad. I've been clearing minefields in Egypt, then I spent some time with my old friends. One of them's a cat and the other one's blind, but it was good. How about you?"

"Meh. After we finished the Cambodia project, DOLAC moved on to South America. But my husband didn't like me being gone all the time. He said I spent more time with my dogs than with him. So, I quit working for DOLAC and got a job. But it turns out that when you live together, you fight a lot. Then his girlfriend got pregnant, and he left.

"At first, I didn't know what to do with myself, but then I heard that the army needed dog handlers, so I enlisted. I called your contractor, and he said you're available, so there we are. I'm so glad to see you, Rambo!"

I didn't get that, other than she was glad to see me, but I wagged my tail.

"Boy, am I happy to see you. You look fantastic. And how's everyone? Frieda, Greta, Gogol? They saved my life that night, you know. I miss them so!"

"Greta and Gogol are good. Brian took them with him for their next project."

"And Frieda?"

"Frieda was an old girl."

My heart skipped a beat. Frieda? Was?

"She got wounded the night you did. She got an infection, and we tried everything, but she was too frail and couldn't shake it off. We had to put her down."

I froze.

"Frieda, gone?"

The night she saved me, she fought Hyena, then took me back to camp. When I was too weak to walk, and she dragged me in, she was already wounded with the wound that would kill her.

I choked with sorrow.

She saved my life, and I killed her.

"That's horrible."

Ash sighed.

"Yes, it was. And where we're going won't be fun either."

**26**

———

She was right.

When we finally stopped in the middle of nowhere, my ears wouldn't stop ringing after hours in that roaring truck that stumbled from one pothole to another. I had panted so much that my tongue stuck to the roof of my mouth, coated in dust. I tried to swallow, but I was out of juice. The heat and the wind had parched me to the core.

Ash opened my crate. I crawled out and tried to jump off, but my legs were so numb I landed on my head.

I waited for the stars to settle. What an entrance! Or was it an exit? Thank Dog, no one saw me.

I scrambled back to my feet, shook off the dust, and found myself staring into the curious eyes of two dogs: a tan Malinois and a red springer.

The Malinois' coat was marred with scratches, and I could tell by the curve of his back and the clouds in his eyes that he was no longer young. His dark face with burning amber eyes looked just like Arco's, but for the flat ears telling me he was worried. About me? But why?

I put that on hold to check his companion.

She was petite and curly, with luxurious pancake ears hanging down to her shoulders and soft, molten chocolate eyes. And what a sassy tail! This chick was the best-looking bitch I've ever seen — sorry, Frieda, Greta, and Cersei. She was top-model material and belonged on the cover of *Dogue* rather than this Dog-forsaken barrack in the desert. I couldn't imagine what she was doing here, but I didn't have time to ponder. The Malinois stepped forward and wrinkled his muzzle, uncovering a yellow but otherwise impressive set of fangs.

I wasn't sure if that was a smile or a warning. I wondered if he and Red Fur had something going on.

"Hello. I'm Viper. This is Lovely," he growled.

I wagged my tail.

"Glad to meet you guys. I'm Rambo."

I offered my butt in a polite introduction. They took their time and sniffed every detail of my CV, schedule, and diet before I got my turn.

I checked Lovely first. She was young, barely a pup, but she had more fight in her than the whole Dutch soccer team at the 2019 Nations League. She was a firecracker. No wonder she kept the old Belgian on his toes. Too bad she was spayed.

Viper's scent reminded me of Frieda's. It wasn't the same — he wasn't a German shepherd, or a female. But he had the same sense of duty, work ethic, and dogged determination. And he was just as grumpy.

Sniffing Viper's butt melted my heart. Oh, how I missed Frieda! And, just like that, Viper won a place in my heart, even though he was Belgian, and we, Dutch, have a complicated relationship with our Belgian neighbors. They're our perennial rivals, so we always try to one-up each other. And Viper knew it, of course.

"Where are you from?"

I wagged my tail respectfully.

"I'm Dutch."

His hackles rose, and his teeth came out a little more. It wasn't hard to see he didn't like me, but Lovely was mesmerized. She came closer to study me, and Viper's scent turned sour.

I felt put on the spot, so I tucked my tail between my legs, but Lovely couldn't care less. She studied my coat like it was a knitting pattern she planned to copy.

"What color are you, if you don't mind my asking?"

"I'm golden brindle. Some of us are silver brindle, but we're all striped. It's a breed requirement."

Viper growled.

"What a stupid thing. What difference does the color make? We, Malinois, can be any color we want, as long as we do our job. It's what's inside that matters."

He glared at me again, then turned away, and my heart plummeted. I'd just arrived in Kandahar, the one place I hoped to never be, and before I even got to step inside, my new partner called me stupid and treated me like dirt.

But why? What did I do?

Oh well. It is what it is. I looked for Ash, but I couldn't see her, so I waved my tail goodbye and followed her scent. I was almost out of range when I heard Lovely growl.

"Oh, Viper. You always find something interesting to say."

I wondered what she meant. I glanced back.

Viper's tail was tucked between his legs, and his ears had flattened into the helicopter look.

I don't know what Lovely meant, but I don't think it was a compliment.

## 27

It didn't take me long to see that Guinness was right. Kandahar was no joke. The dust and the heat were no fun, and the locals didn't like us one bit.

But it wasn't all bad.

Lovely was lots of fun. Unlike shepherds, whose best jokes are about pulling your tail, Springers do have a sense of humor.

It was great to be back with Ash, and looking for IEDs was way more interesting than clearing mines because you never knew what to expect. More dangerous too. Unlike Cambodia, where once you cleared a mine, it was gone for good, these IEDs kept coming. You could make the same trip a hundred times and still find new devices. There was no safety outside the razor wire.

But the biggest difference was in the people. The Khmers learned to like us and became our friends. But the Afghans hated us. All of them, from the old to the young. There were no fried tarantulas, no spicy crickets, not even chicken bones. And nobody ever came to watch us work.

Maybe because we went to them?

Most days, we went to look for explosives, weapons, and ammunition in their villages, their homes, and even on their bodies. We'd scour the compound and the mud huts, looking for anything smelling like explosives as they watched. Their clenched fists and burning eyes told us loud and clear that they wanted us dead.

That's why I missed the Khmers. But I missed Cambodia even more.

Gone were the rain and the mud. Gone were the monkeys fighting over bananas, the birds waking us up at dawn with their cackling, and the blood-curdling screams of the elephants at night. Gone were the creepy crawlies we loved to chase. Gone were the jungle, the muddy rice fields, and the grass.

This place is dry as an old bone. There's nothing but orange desert, and the dust never settles. The heat relents at night, but the scorching starts over when the first rays of sun peep through the windows.

We, K-9s, share a hangar with the soldiers, our crates at one end, their cots at the other, and I love watching them.

Besides my weeks with Mike, I've never spent much time with humans since I only lived in kennels. That's why I find them fascinating, from how they take off their boots — Mike's came off with his feet — to how they chew that evil thing called gum that almost killed me. Da insisted I try it, and I did, but it glued my mouth shut. Thankfully, Ash unclenched my mouth and took it out.

I was napping once when the men playing with pieces of cardboard started screaming. I thought we were under attack, and I jumped up, but they burst into laughter.

"What in Dog's name are they doing?"

Lovely opened an eye.

"Playing cards. You haven't seen that before?"

"Never. What does that mean?"

"I don't know. But something about it gives them joy. Or pain. They even did that in jail."

"You were in jail?"

"For training. How about you? Where did you live before?"

"In kennels."

"It shows," Viper growled, turning his back to his untouched dinner.

That was the only thing he said all night. Viper didn't talk much and never to me. He still didn't like me one bit, and that started way before I found those boots he missed. He'd been crabby since the day I arrived.

I wondered why, until I smelled his misery whenever I got near Lovely. He wanted her all to himself; that's why he didn't want me here. Well, it wasn't like I had a choice, but I did my best to stay away from her.

It didn't help. Viper had aged a ton in the last few weeks. He got slower, clumsier, and grumpier every day, and it hurt to see him fall apart.

"I don't know what's wrong with him. Ever since you arrived, he's been a changed dog," Lovely growled.

That broke my heart, and I wished I could help. But I didn't know how.

Then, like that wasn't bad enough, Prozac came.

That's when we knew Viper was a goner.

**28**

———

Lovely and I sat shoulder to shoulder and watched our new partner tumble off the dusty truck. The new K-9 was a shaggy floppy-eared orange, looking like Cersei's twin. I could bet a fresh cow femur against a rolled newspaper that he was a golden retriever.

"What's up with that?" I growled.

"What's up with what?" Lovely asked.

The two of us had rushed out to greet our new partner. That's the civil thing to do since the new recruits know nothing about the camp, not even where to check their peemail. Sure, they can sniff it out — we're scent dogs, after all. But making him feel welcome was the right thing to do. And we couldn't wait to meet him. There isn't much excitement inside the wire, and new folks always bring news about the world.

Lovely did her best to drag Viper out, but he didn't want to leave his crate.

"Come on, Viper! Aren't you curious to see what breed the new K-9 is? And get to know him?"

Viper turned to his other side.

"You two are enough of a welcome committee. And I'll have plenty of time to know him better than I care to."

It turned out he was wrong. But that was later. For now, Lovely and I stared at the new K-9, wondering what to make of him.

Lovely nudged me.

"What's up with what?"

She's always like that. Like a dog with a bone, she just won't give up.

"What's up with all these floppy-eared dogs in the scent business?" I blurted; then I wished I hadn't.

Lovely scowled at me.

"I beg your pardon?"

"I'm sorry, Lovely, but I still remember when the Scent Dog Club was pointy-eared exclusive. Nobody but Dutch shepherds, German shepherds, and Malinois. But these days, they'll let any floppy-eared..."

Lovely wrinkled her muzzle and flashed her white fangs.

"You were saying?"

I stared at her red ears that rested on her shoulders and bit my tongue. Too late, of course.

"I didn't mean you. I just wondered..."

"Wondered what?"

"Why all these floppy-ear breeds? Not like they have better noses or a better work ethic."

There. I did it.

Lovely shook her head until her ears slapped her muzzle, then looked at me down her long, shapely nose.

"Fact #1: I do have a better nose than either you or Viper. Fact #2: I may not be a workaholic like you two, but I always do my job."

I shut my mouth and flattened my ears, but she was on a roll.

"You, pointy-eared breeds, think WAY too highly about yourselves. There's no end to how many ways a cuddly, floppy-eared scent dog works better than you pointy-eared maniacs. Like sniffing people in airports, marathons, and mass events. Meeting kids in schools and visiting hospitals."

"What does that have to do with sniffing?" I blurted, then tucked my tail between my legs.

But it was too late. Lovely lifted her nose up in the air like I stank and abandoned me to meet the new K-9. I followed her, wishing I'd kept my mouth shut. I knew I'd pay for this, but hopefully not before our new partner, so I decided to stick to him for dear life.

Lovely wagged her tail, and Orange Dog offered his butt in introduction. She proceeded to sniff it, and I joined in.

Yep, he's a golden, and he's not young. He ate rice lamb formula with glucosamine and chondroitin, which probably means he's got bad hips. But other than that — and the floppy ears — he smells competent, confident, and friendly.

He sniffs our butts; then we touch each other's noses.

"I'm Lovely. This is Rambo."

"Good to meet you guys. I'm Prozac. Some call me ProZak. Zak to my friends."

Lovely wags her tail.

"What a unique name! I love it!"

"I bet so does Big Pharma," Viper growls.

He decided to come out after all, but he can't help being grumpy. Prozac glances at him and jumps back like he's seen a ghost.

"Jinx? Is that you?"

"No. I'm Viper, Jinx's twin."

Isn't that interesting! I can't wait to hear more, but Lovely nudges me away.

"Let's go inside."

"But..."

"No 'but.' Let's go."

I follow her with my tail between my legs. I know she made me miss this exciting conversation to jump on me about my unfortunate floppy-eared comments.

But fortunately, the whole hangar boils with excitement, and she forgets. The men buzz around, bumping into each other like a hive of frazzled bees.

"What's up?" Lovely asks Brown, her handler.

"We're getting ready for Viper's retirement party. He's leaving tomorrow."

I wag my tail.

"Good for him."

Lovely wrinkles her nose and flashes her gleaming white teeth.

"Viper can't retire."

"Why not? He's getting old. He has a hard time keeping up, and he makes mistakes. And Dog knows he's paid his dues. Isn't it time he gets to lay on his sofa and chill with his family?" I say, remembering Frieda like I do every day. The old girl missed her retirement, thanks to me. I hope Viper fares better.

Lovely glowers at me like I'm an IED.

"Viper can't retire. He has no sofa, no family, and no home to go to. Viper has no place to go."

## 29

---

"What do you mean he has no place to go? But..."

"But what? Where would you go if they sent you home tomorrow?"

Where would I go? I left Holland so long ago that it's no longer home. Cambodia and Angola were only work. The closest thing I have to a home would be with Cersei and Tyrion. But would Mike want me back?

"I don't know. How about you?"

"I don't know either. But this isn't about you or me; it's about Viper. We need to..."

But I didn't get what we needed to do because Viper and Prozac came in, and the humans started cheering and clapping. They queued to pet Viper, and young Dan even hugged him. Viper's ears went so flat I thought they'd fall off.

He sat hunched with his tail between his legs, listening to the lieutenant's speech. Then they gave him an ugly tag, which is some Dickin medal they give to cats and pigeons. Then they told him he was going to the family of his last handler — the one nobody missed when the Taliban killed him.

Lovely gasped.

"That's terrible! Dick was a lousy human. He made everyone's life miserable — Viper's, mine, even Brown's. And now they'll send Viper to live with his family? We need to stop that."

Prozac shook his head.

"I wonder how. Humans don't often make sense, but the army is worse. When it makes a decision, there's no stopping it. It's like a truck heading downhill on broken brakes."

Lovely growled and mumbled and threatened to strike, but Prozac was right. There was no stopping it.

We sat with heavy hearts and watched Viper's truck get swallowed by the dust. His sad eyes and the stench of his despair will stay with me until the day I die. If that's retirement, I want no part of it. It made me wonder if Frieda was the lucky one.

But life went on, and we had work to do.

Prozac, Lovely, and I took turns leading the daily patrols. It wasn't hard once you learned to ignore the heat, the dust, and the ever-present stench of hate. And finding IEDs was even fun!

But it could get tricky.

The day I found an IED just by the village compound wall, I sat and pointed it out to Ash, as usual. She finger-swept the dust and confirmed it, and I felt pretty proud of myself.

Then Lovely barked from the rear.

"It's a trap."

"What?"

"That IED is a trap meant to keep us here. Let's turn around and head back."

What? Just leave that darn thing here and leave? Then what's the point of searching for it in the first place?

I stared at Ash. She shrugged.

I wondered if Lovely had lost it, but Brown, her handler, called.

"Let's head back. Now!"

The other humans stared at him in disbelief, but he insisted.

"Let's go!"

It took us a while to head back because none of us could believe we'd just leave that IED there and turn around for no good reason. But that's precisely what we did.

We trudged back one after the other, following Lovely, who cleared the way. The silence was so deep it hurt. Besides the heat and the dust, that's one more thing about the desert. The silence. The jungle's never quiet, but the desert is so empty that there's nobody there to make noise. No monkeys, no elephants, no crickets. Not even tarantulas. There are no rivers to bubble or waterfalls to cascade. Not even tree leaves to rustle in the wind. The desert is nothing but silence, orange dust, and the bloody sun sucking the life out of you.

We shuffled behind Lovely and Brown, step after weary step, and nothing happened. I looked back. Nothing but the dust we raised. And the silence.

Lovely's confident stride slowed down to a shuffle. The more nothing happened, the more her tail squeezed between her legs, and the lower her head hung. She knew she'd messed up. I can't imagine what Brown was thinking, following her cues and aborting our mission?

Oh well. We'd be back tomorrow. I already knew where that IED was, so finding it would be a breeze.

When the green gate screeched open, Lovely's march had stalled to a crawl.

Then the earth shook.

I'd seen IEDs blow up and heard my share of weapons fire. But never that kind of thunder, nor a quake like that. It was like the mother of all IEDs had exploded. It mushroomed the desert into a cloud of dust that turned the pale blue sky into sick orange.

We dropped to take cover and waited for the dust to settle. I looked back. A hole as big as a truck sat right where Ash and I had been. The compound wall and the mud houses behind it had crumbled into dust. Like Ash and I would have if Lovely hadn't called off the mission.

"But how did you know? You couldn't have smelled anything; you were too far," I asked.

Prozac agreed.

"Yes, really. How did you know?"

Lovely wagged her tail.

"I remembered Viper. His hackles always went up by that corner. He taught me not to trust that spot. 'That's the worst place in this desert, Lovely. Don't trust it. Nothing good ever came from behind that wall. That's where Butter got shot and Silver, Guinness' handler, got killed. Don't linger there, even if you don't smell, hear, or see anything.'

"So when you found that IED, I knew something wasn't right. Why would they plant an IED so close it would destroy their compound? They did it to trap us."

Wow. Just wow. I'd always known that Lovely was more than a pretty tail, but I didn't know she was THAT good.

I licked her nose.

"Thanks for saving my life, partner. I'm proud to be on your team!"

Too bad it didn't last.

**30**

———

It wasn't Lovely's fault she got hurt. If anything, that fabulous nose of hers saved her life.

We were on patrol, as usual. But this time, Lovely cleared our way out of the Afghan compound as I watched the rear. I was a hundred feet behind her when I saw her lift her muzzle to the sky, sniff something, and then recoil like she'd stepped on hot coals. That jump must have saved her life.

It wasn't Prozac's fault either.

He'd sniffed something funky in the hut he was checking. He called Cho, his handler, but she dismissed it. We moved on, but I could tell by Prozac's droopy tail that he wasn't happy.

We headed back to the base. We weren't quite past that darned compound when something exploded. Lovely flew up in the air, then landed on her head and fell asleep.

We couldn't wake her up no matter what, though Dog knows we tried. We barked in her ears, licked her nose, and even bit her tail, but nothing helped. Even when Brown and Ash stuck needles in her legs and tied her to some funky tubes, she lay there snoring. I'd be darned if it didn't look like she'd sleep forever.

We went nuts with worry. The lieutenant even called a helicopter to take her to the hospital, but the weather was so bad that nothing could fly but the birds.

Then, just as the weather got better, she woke up.

Brown checked every inch of her. Prozac and I did too. We sniffed her butt, tasted her nose, and watched her every move. But everything looked fine, so we figured she was just tired.

But the next day, when we went to train, Lovely missed Brown's decoy.

We thought she was kidding. That chick may be small and cute, but she's got a springer's nose that neither Prozac nor I could match.

But it turns out she wasn't. She went through the whole field twice and didn't find it.

Lovely had lost her nose.

We froze.

For a dog, losing his sense of smell is worse than losing his eyes or ears, give or take a leg. Dogs are planned like that. Our noses let us make sense of the world. That's how we recognize one another, read each other's feelings, and communicate. That's even how we make some sense of humans, Dog help them. There's nothing more important for a dog than his nose.

But Lovely isn't any dog; she's an explosive-detecting K-9. Her nose is not just social; it's essential equipment for her job. How could she sniff explosives, clear terrain, or track someone's scent on a gun without it? A dog without his nose is lost, and an explosive-detecting K-9 is useless. And Lovely was both.

Prozac and I wanted to help, but we didn't know how. So we crowded her and sniffed her, looking for answers, until she flashed her teeth, telling us to back off. So we did.

She never complained, but we could smelled her despair. And we felt lost.

"What would you do if you lost your nose?" I asked Prozac one day when Brown took Lovely out to train her, like she had anything to work with. But she couldn't even read the peemail or smell dinner, for Dog's sake!

Prozac shuddered.

"I dunno, Ram. I can't even imagine it. I'm almost eight, you know, and my eyes are no longer like they used to be. My hips hurt, and even my stomach got iffy. I remember when I could eat a whole chicken, bones and all, and look for more. Not anymore. I stole a chicken wing the other day. I scarfed it, then it took me two hours to puke it out. Losing my nose would mean losing everything I enjoy: tasting my food, sniffing the bushes for stories, exchanging news with a friend. I wouldn't want to live without my nose. But Lovely is not an old dog like me; she's just a pup. You must be about her age."

"I think I'm four or five. She may be three. But I don't think our nose has much to do with age. They say that's the one part of a dog that never gets old. That, and the heart. But I'd be devastated if I lost my nose. I can't imagine what I'd do with myself. What good would I be without my nose?"

Prozac shook his head.

"None of us would be much good without our nose. And here, in the army, they don't keep you unless you're useful. Remember Viper? And he was still doing good work."

"You think they'll send Lovely home too?"

Prozac sighed.

"I dunno, Ram. Sending K-9s home is complicated. You need crates and trucks and planes, and Dog knows what else. And money, whatever they use that for. Plus, a home that wants them. Does Lovely have a home?"

"She said something about prison. And Brown's home, but Brown is here. You think they'll try to get her adopted like they did with Viper?"

Prozac yawned. I didn't like it.

"Viper was a veteran and a hero. He didn't have much time left.

But Lovely's just a pup — she may live another ten years. If they let her."

"If they let her? What do you mean?"

"They may decide it's easier to just put her down. That's what they did with the military dogs when they left Vietnam. They called it euthanizing, but that's just a fancy way to say kill."

**31**

---

A few days later, Prozac and I sit in the yard watching the truck wait for Lovely. Her crate is already loaded. So is her water bowl and the silly little Kong she chews on when she's deep in thought. Lovely never had a real Kong like Viper and me because she preferred treats as a reward.

Until she lost her nose. After that, there'd been no more rewards. No Kong and no treats, because she never found another IED.

I swallow the knot in my throat. The little one was so proud of her nose. She worked so hard to show us, big dogs, that she was just as good, if not better. And now...

I sniff. Prozac yawns. We keep waiting.

She took Brown for a walk before getting locked in that crate for Dog knows how long. Prozac and I wanted to join them, but Ash held us back.

"No. This is Lovely's last time with Brown. Let them say goodbye."

My heart sank.

"You think?"

"Well, miracles sometimes happen. But until then, I think this is his last time with Lovely."

My stomach turns, and I yawn like I always do when I hurt.

"So, you think this is it for Lovely?"

Ash shrugs.

"You never know. They say even the dead can come back. But I think this is it."

She's so casual she gets me get rattled. I study her from the her blonde head to the dusty toes of her boots, wondering if I even know this human. She gave her MRE to Lovely that day she saved our lives, but now she speaks like her death is no big deal. My hackles go up.

"Aren't you angry?"

"Angry? Why?"

"For losing such a great K-9."

"I'm more sad than angry. But there's nothing we can do but hope and pray."

I get so mad I want to sink my teeth in her. But I don't. I just twist three times, precisely 720 degrees, and lay with Prozac to wait for Lovely. But she's taking her time.

"You think this is it?"

Prozac cocks his head.

"I don't know, Ram. Brown said they'll send her to some fancy hospital to fix her nose. But I wonder if he's just saying that to make her feel better."

That's not what I hoped to hear. But there she is, bringing Brown to the gate for the last time. Her head up, her red ears floating behind, she's dancing on her feet like she's late for a party.

Prozac and I try to look happy, but we're both lousy liars. I wag my tail and struggle to perk up my ears, but, as nose-blind as she is, Lovely can see we're miserable.

"Come on, boys! I'll be all right. I'll just go get these little white pills to fix my nose, and I'll be back in no time. You two hold the fort while I'm gone. And look after Brown. He's such a klutz he can't find his own stinky socks without help, let alone find IEDs. Take care of him for me, will you?"

I struggle to keep my ears from flattening into my gloomy helicopter look. Prozac's got it easy since his ears flop anyhow, but he sighs and pretends to be sneezing.

"Come on, boys! Before long, we'll go search for IEDs again. But take care while I'm gone. No casualties, OK?"

I want to bark, "yes," but my throat is too tight, so I just wag my tail. Prozac growls.

"We'll take care of Brown and each other, but you take care of yourself. We're worried sick about you, all alone like that, with no one to look after you. What if... what if something happens?"

Lovely wags her tail.

"Are you kidding? Nothing bad can happen to me; I'm pre-disastered. But you two better look after each other, you hear me?"

She bursts with joy, and I'm glad she can't smell us. We're terrified about what will happen to her, but she thinks we're just sad to see her go.

"Bye, guys. See you soon."

We lick her nose, then Brown lifts her into her crate and locks her in.

The truck growls and takes off.

Prozac and I stand shoulder to shoulder, watching Lovely get swallowed by the dust. It's just like Viper not long ago, and our hearts break again.

"You think she'll return?" I ask again. I know he doesn't know, but I need him to lie to me. Just this once.

Zak shakes his head.

"Dog willing."

**32**

———

And just like that, we went from four K-9 teams to two, faster than you could catch your tail. Then the Taliban went crazy, and that didn't help one bit. We patrolled every day, taking turns in the lead, and we always found something, whether IEDs, weapons, or ammunition. And the more we found, the more we looked.

But the scorching heat, the endless dust, and the never-ending hate got to us. We were drained. Spending day after day in that hell did a number on your brain, not only your body. I was just four, and I felt exhausted. I wondered how Prozac managed to hold on.

He never complained, but his steps got smaller, his walk slower, and his back curved more every day. I smelled his pain, and I wished I could help, but there was no rest for any of us.

One night, the alarm woke us up before sunrise, and I thought we were under attack. But it was just the lieutenant briefing the soldiers. I didn't get much of what he said, but I knew something was off from his rancid smell and their long faces.

"We're going on a special mission."

The soldiers grumbled, their voices hoarse from sleep.

"What's new?"

"The aerial surveillance blimps found unusual activity in the mountains, about 20 miles northwest from here. The Taliban are preparing a massive spring offensive, so they've been gathering weapons and ammunition to fuel it. Our intelligence points to a cave in the mountains where they built a large cache of arms that could cost us and our allies hundreds of lives. Our mission is to find and destroy it."

The air turned rank and stank of dread.

Emil cleared his throat.

"You're kidding, yes?"

"Not in the least."

Emil sighed.

"Listen, Lieutenant. I don't think I need to tell you, but driving twenty miles into enemy territory is a terrible idea. There's no shelter other than here and no way to keep this secret. It will take hours to drive there over these potholed roads, even if they weren't mined. The Taliban will know our every move as soon as we open the gates, and they'll be waiting."

"You're right, Emil. You don't need to tell me. Anyone else?"

Brown shook his head.

"That's the worst thing I heard ever since we manned that checkpoint looking for a weapons transport. We lost Viper's handler in that carnage. Abdul, our translator, lost a hand, and God only knows how many Afghans died. Whose bright idea was this?"

The lieutenant's eyes narrowed.

"Not mine. As you know, this is the army. We receive orders, and we obey them. Any other questions?"

"What do we do when we find the weapons?" Dan asked.

Emil laughed.

"What an optimist. IF we find them. There's every chance we'll die first."

The lieutenant scowled.

"You will be told when necessary. Let's go. Cho and Prozac, you're leading today."

The air stank of fear and worry, but nobody spoke as the men donned their equipment: bulky bulletproof vests, heavy helmets, goggles, and tons of weapons and ammunition.

Ash's hands shook as she clipped my bulletproof vest.

"We'll be OK, Rambo. Don't worry."

I knew she spoke to herself as much as she talked to me, so I licked her cold fingers to make her feel better. She touched her nose to mine.

The clanging of metal against metal shattered the night's silence. Heavy boots pounded the ground. One by one, we loaded into the truck. The gates screeched open, the engine roared, and the tires bit the gravel and spat it behind. Heartbeats later, we're on the road, leaving safety behind.

We're well on our way when the sky turns red. A red sun peeks behind the black mountains that stick up like hungry fangs, dripping blood over the desert.

I shiver.

Prozac leans against my shoulder.

"It's OK, Rambo. It's just another mission. The sunrise is red, of course — they all are. We're in the desert."

I lean into him, grateful for his wisdom and glad he's by my side.

And, for some reason, I remember Lovely. It's been months since she left, and we never heard a word. I don't know if that's good or bad, and I'm afraid to ask. But right now, I'm glad she's not here. Bad enough that Prozac and I are. I hope she's somewhere safe.

"Thanks, Zak. You're right. It's just another desert sunrise. That red sky doesn't mean anything. We'll be back."

Prozac's kind eyes look into mine, and he licks my nose.

"You will, Ram. But I won't. This is my last mission."

## 33

My heart froze.

"What..."

The truck stopped with a jolt, throwing us forward. The driver cut the engine, and the silence swallowed us like fog. The soldiers jumped out, one after the other, stumbling under the weight of their equipment, and we followed.

"This ain't the desert," Brown mumbled, tightening his bullet-proof vest around him.

He was right. No more orange dirt, just peak after jagged peak of sharp rock pointing to the sky, ready to bite. Skeletal trees shook, squeaked, and moaned, tortured by the wind, shivering through their skinny needles. A pained scream sliced the air like a knife. Another one answered.

Ash shivered.

"That's got to be some sort of bird."

"I've never ever heard anything like that," Cho whispered.

Neither had I. Not even in Cambodia, where all living things, from birds to elephants, love to howl, screech, and holler through the night.

The dry heat was gone. This wind had a bite, and its chill made me shiver. Unless it was Prozac's words. I wanted to ask him what he meant, but I didn't get to.

"Let's go," the lieutenant murmured, his voice so soft I barely heard him.

But if he tried to hide our presence, he was too late.

The enemy was there. I couldn't hear, see, or even smell them, but I felt them. I felt the wave of poisonous hate coming at us from the mountains, and I wished we were somewhere else.

"Go where?" Brown asked.

The lieutenant glanced at his watch.

"Northwest. It shouldn't be more than a mile or so. Cho and Prozac, you go first. Ash and Rambo, you're last. Watch our back. The last thing we need is to get surrounded. If you see or hear anything behind us, let me know. Brown, you follow Prozac and Cho in case they need help. Everyone else, you know your place. Let's go. The sooner we find this darn place, the sooner we can leave, OK? I want no casualties today."

"What do we do when we find it?" Dan asked again.

The lieutenant frowned.

"I'll let you know when you do. Now go!"

We lined up behind Prozac and Cho, as usual, but everything was different. This wasn't the desert, wide open as far as the eye could see, where we filed to step in each other's steps. This was nothing but scrambling up and down rocks, crawling under trees, and sneaking around the boulders blocking the goat path.

I watched Prozac climb. His hips were so stiff his back curved, but his tail was up like a flag, and he never relented. I wished I could take his place, but it was his turn in the lead. All I could do was watch his back to tell him if badness was coming. That was hard. My old friend faced dangers like we hadn't seen before, and I could do nothing but watch.

"Zak!"

"What?"

"Take your time, old boy! Don't rush! You wouldn't want to mess your orange do!"

Prozac snorted.

"Back at you, brindle warrior! Take it easy. Don't strain!"

We were kidding, of course. That was our roundabout way to tell each other how much we cared.

Cho followed Zak, quiet as a ghost. Stumbling and cursing, Brown followed Cho.

"This is insane. I bet you every Taliban, from the oldest to the youngest, knows we're here. They're only waiting for us to get in even deeper before they jump us. What the heck are we here for? This is not our kind of operation! This is what special-ops ninjas do. They should parachute them here in the dark to blow up that cache."

"Shut up, Brown. Keep your mouth shut and your legs moving if you want to get out alive."

Brown spat to the side and said nothing more, but even I knew he was right.

"I wonder if they sent us here as a decoy. To distract the Taliban from what the special-ops are doing," Emil said.

Brown nodded.

"Now that would make some sense, wouldn't it."

The climb became too rough to talk. We needed our breaths to clamber up that miserable path. Boulders blocked the way; pebbles rolled under boots, hitting the men behind; rocks shifted, throwing people off balance. The climb was hard, slow, and painful.

But Prozac and Cho kept going. We watched them scale rock after rock and lost sight of them as they dipped into ravines to reappear on the other side. We followed them, slinking our way up that mountain like a giant caterpillar.

I kept my eyes and nose open, sniffing every way but forward. That was the one way I didn't need to worry about since our men were there. But other than that, the enemy could come from anywhere. And I knew it was coming; I just didn't know when.

The lieutenant stopped to recheck his watch.

"We should be there by now. I wonder if we missed it."

He was still staring at his watch when Zak's howl shredded the silence, making the mountains tremble.

I looked up. Nothing but the sky, so blue it looked fake, and the threatening mountain. The rocks threw shadows as dark as night against the bright sun, and I saw nothing. No enemy, no animals, no birds.

No Prozac and no Cho.

Nothing but that ominous warning telling me that something terrible was coming.

That was the call of my people. I knew it, even though I'd never heard it. My heart froze.

I lifted my muzzle to the sky and howled back to Zak that I got it. Then I barked.

"Zak? Are you there?"

"Zak?"

The first gunshot sounded like thunder. The next echoed between the peaks like a storm.

The soldiers dropped to the ground and returned fire. But this wasn't the flat, dusty desert we knew. This was the mountain, and we didn't know it. Shots coming from above trapped us in our rock prisons. We took shelter, wishing for the desert dust to hide us.

The gunfire picked up, fast and furious. Someone threw a grenade, and the blast echoed from one peak to another like forever. Stone chips and rocks flew over my head like bullets, and I melted into the ground.

Another grenade blasted the rock hiding Dan, and he screamed and screamed. His agonizing wails turned my stomach. A bullet hit the crackling radio, exploding it into a thousand pieces. Someone to my left returned fire; far above, someone screamed. Another string of rapid-fire, then someone cursed, and I knew it was Brown.

The air thickened with smoke and powder, and the fumes

burned my nose. A grenade dropped to my right, and Ash screamed.

I followed the scent of her blood and crawled to look for her. She'd sheltered in a dip between rocks, holding her hands around her bleeding knee. She let go of it to get her first-aid kit, and a stream of blood spurted into the sky. A bullet whizzed by and hit the rock behind me. Ash sobbed and grabbed her knee again.

I crawled and pulled out her first-aid kit from her vest and dropped it in her lap. She grabbed the snake-like rubber ribbon and tightened it around her leg. The bleeding slowed to a trickle.

I lifted my nose to sniff for Prozac and Cho and got nothing but the stench of blood and gunpowder. And fear. And pain. Someone up there was hurting, and I hoped it wasn't Zac. The only way to know was to find him.

I started crawling up.

"No, Rambo! They'll kill you!" Ash shouted.

But I had to find Prozac.

A bullet flew above my head as I jumped from one rock to the next, then clawed my way between two stones to the next shelter.

That had been Dan's. His hands held his weapon, and his blue eyes watched the sky, but his heart had stopped beating.

"What will we do when we find them?" he'd asked.

He'll never know.

I pushed forward. I crawled low, taking the sheltered path in the narrow places where the bullets couldn't find me. Always upwards.

A grenade exploded to my right, raining a hail of rocks and shards over me. I pushed forward.

A massive boulder cut my way, lodged between two stone walls.

I glanced left and right. There was no other way.

I leaped, then clawed up, digging my claws into the mossy rock.

I slid back.

I leaped again, pushing hard with my hind paws. I scaled the boulder and then jumped off as fast as I could.

Not fast enough.

Mind-numbing pain seared my hip as I tumbled forward and hit the ground headfirst. I stopped to breathe.

"You OK, bud?" Brown asked. He'd curled behind two boulders and wedged his weapon between them, looking for targets.

But I didn't get to answer. The world went nuts.

I'd been too busy to hear the helicopters, but now their growl covered the gunshots, and their downdraft almost stripped off my coat.

They opened fire. The mountain shivered, the sky trembled, and the enemy vanished. It was hell; then it was over. Just heartbeats later, the fight was over, and the enemy was gone.

But the pain had only just begun. It was time to care for our wounded and count our dead.

Dan was gone. The poor kid will never get to be a dog handler or see if his magic acne solution made a difference.

Ash's leg was barely bleeding, but it looked shattered, and she couldn't stand.

Brown's wound was just a scratch. Same with my hip, though it hurt like the dickens. The others had scrapes, sprains, and bruises.

The lieutenant sighed.

"This is terrible, but it could have been worse. One dead, one wounded, but the rest look OK."

Brown frowned.

"But..."

"But, what?"

"Where are Cho and Prozac?"

Prozac and Cho were gone.

**34**

———

The trip back to the base took forever. The soldiers sat hugging their knees without a word, all gray with fatigue and stinking of grief. The odor of gunpowder, blood, and fear was so thick it choked me.

I sat all alone between their feet. I missed Prozac's shoulder next to mine, his confident smell, the sound of his heart giving me strength.

How did he know? How did he know this would be his last mission?

We looked for him and Cho, but all we found was a handful of Zak's fur clinging to dried blood splatter and Cho's broken goggles.

Brown examined the blood and shook his head.

"This looks like an arterial bleed. Or gunshot splatter. Either way, it's bad."

"But where the heck can they be?" Emil asked.

"The Taliban took them. Whether dead or alive, we don't know."

"They've got to be alive. Why would the Taliban bother to carry two dead bodies, one of them a dog, through these God-forsaken mountains?"

"For PR. Have you seen their videos? Nothing is too much for them. If Cho and Prozac are alive, they'll parade and humiliate them to show their strength and embarrass us. If they're dead, they'll display and disgrace them to demean us all. Either way, it's a PR coup. 'Thanks to Allah and our men's bravery, we captured a K-9 special-ops team. Look at them cower.' "

"That's sick."

"Yep. But efficient."

All I got was Prozac's name, so I barked to call him.

"Zak! Buddy! Where are you?"

The mountains barked back, but it was just the echo, laughing at me. I opened my mouth to call again, but Brown tightened his hands around my muzzle.

"Shhh! You don't want the enemy to come back, do you?"

"Like they don't know we're here already," Emil mumbled.

So we looked and looked, but left without them.

I missed Prozac like I missed a limb. And I missed Ash.

I lay next to her as we waited for the medevac, feeling her pain. I licked her fingers. She rubbed my ears.

"I'll miss you, Rambo!"

I wagged my tail.

"Miss me? Not at all. I'm not going anywhere."

She wiped her eyes.

The medevac came, noisier than a dozen trucks and windy enough to suck me in. I followed Ash's stretcher and tried to jump after her, but Brown held me back.

"Sorry, Rambo, you can't go. They're taking her to the hospital."

"But..."

"She'll be all right, Ram. Come on. Let's go."

I watched the helicopter grow smaller and smaller until it vanished in the clouds, and my heart sank. I'd lost her again.

We headed back down. Brown and I cleared the path; the others shuffled behind us, tired and weary. We checked every rock and peeked inside every crevasse, expecting an attack. But the helicopter hovering above us must have kept them at bay.

Brown shook his head.

"What a terrible day. Dan is dead, Cho and Prozac missing, and Ash is gone. Can it get any worse?"

It turned out it could.

$$35$$

More bad days followed.

With Ash, Prozac, and Cho gone, I was the only K-9 left and Brown the only handler, so we teamed together.

I didn't mind. Brown was big and black and spoke slowly — maybe because he came from the South. And he had strong, gentle hands.

But he wasn't Ash.

I kept hoping she'd return, so every night before dinner, I went to the gate to wait for the truck that came every day bringing mail, supplies, and new recruits. But it never brought Ash.

I sniffed them all as they got off, just in case. Then I tucked my tail between my legs and dragged myself back in. I ate my kibble and curled in my crate for the night. When the morning came, I started waiting for the mail truck again. Then again.

It hurt. But I never got tired of hoping.

Brown understood.

"You miss Ashley, don't you? Me too. I miss her, and Lovely, and Viper. But she'll be OK. She'll be back as soon as she's better, you'll see, though that knee looked terrible. It's gonna take a while to heal. But she's young and strong, and she'll recover. You just wait."

I waited and waited, but Ash didn't return.

I missed Prozac too and kept wondering what happened to him. I hoped he was alive and well somewhere. But wouldn't he come back? Or at least send us word that he's OK?

But how? It's not like he could read and write. Or even text. We K-9s don't write; we just peemail, which doesn't work long-distance.

I missed Lovely too, and I wondered what had happened to her. I could have asked Brown, but I guess I didn't really want to know. I preferred to think that she's OK somewhere rather than find out she's gone.

All in all, I was grumpy, gloomy, and miserable. But I was not the only one. The men were all in a funk, and the camp throbbed with rumors and whispers.

"There's a major Taliban offensive in the North. They say it's just a matter of weeks before the Kabul government falls."

"They started withdrawing the troops. One of my buddies who was deployed in Helmand just got to Germany."

"They say we're leaving any day now. Next week maybe."

The lieutenant didn't like that.

"You all, stop spreading unfounded rumors. They aren't true, and they just ruin the morale," he said.

But there was no stopping them. Everyone listened to the radio or got news from their buddies, and then they talked about it. The camp was deep in gloom.

Until the day the lieutenant gathered them all.

"We're leaving. Get your equipment and your stuff. Whatever's not essential stays behind. You can only take what you can carry. Get ready."

The men stared at him in disbelief.

"But..."

"No 'but.' We have our orders. Get ready."

"When?"

"Tonight."

The stench of fear and loathing fouled the air as they all started filling their backpacks. Brown took his kids' pictures off the wall, rolled them carefully, and packed them with his laptop, bible, and toothbrush. He added two pairs of socks and two t-shirts from his coffer, then shrugged at the rest.

"It is what it is."

I cocked my head.

"What is?"

He sighed.

"We're leaving today, Rambo."

"Where?"

"Darned if I know. Wherever the army sends us, I guess. If we're lucky, we're going back home. If not, maybe Germany. Or Qatar. I don't know. Wherever the plane takes us."

"How about Prozac? And Cho?"

"I don't know, Ram. I doubt they're still alive. But if they are, they're not in a good place. What can I say? It is what it is."

I didn't like that one bit. Not because I wanted to stay — I'd had enough of Kandahar to last me a lifetime and then some. But what if Prozac was still in the mountains? He'd try to escape. And if he did, where could he go but come here? And what if we're gone? After miles and miles of trudging through the mountains and the desert, he comes here to find nothing? After all that struggle?

That can't be.

That night I got in trouble in Cambodia, my buddies risked their lives to save me. Frieda even died. And these humans will just abandon Prozac and leave like he didn't matter?

I got mad.

But what should I do?

Whatever I could.

I went around the camp and left peemails all over the fence to tell him we left, but he should keep safe and follow the truck. Then I went and peed on every wheel to make sure he knew which truck to follow.

I had started running out of juice, so I gulped some water and looked around. The men were busy packing, checking the news, or writing home. So I squeezed into the supply room and ripped open every bag of dog food to make sure they didn't take them, so Prozac could find food when he came.

How about water?

The plastic jugs they mount in the coolers were stacked in the back, but they were far too big for me to carry. And if they locked the supply room, Prozac couldn't get in.

So I climbed on top of the water jug stack and scattered them all over the floor. Then, to be extra sure, I ate the key.

**36**

———

We drove, and drove, and drove, dropping from pothole to pothole, swallowing the dust of the trucks ahead of us and spewing fumes to the ones behind. The men held their weapons ready and their precious packs between their knees. They were packed so tight their knees touched, but nobody said a word.

I sat between their legs and focused on keeping my mouth closed to make sure I didn't bite my tongue. Between the engine's roar and the static of the radio Emil struggled with, my ears never stopped ringing.

The road north was crowded. We'd always been the only truck on the road, but today we were just one out of many. The endless orange desert crawled with trucks trailing behind each other like ants.

"How much longer?" Emil asked.

Brown shrugged.

"Why? You're in a hurry? You have a date or something?"

"I wish. This is terrible."

"What?"

"Leaving like this."

The lieutenant frowned.

"I'll remind you that this war lasted for twenty years. It's been the longest war in American history, but it was bound to end some-time. We can't stay here forever. It's high time to let the Afghans take charge of their country."

"But not like this, bailing out with our tails between our legs! Then what's the point of all the years we spent here? Why did so many of us die or lose their limbs or their minds? To have us rush out, leaving behind all the people who trusted us and tons of equip-ment? Look at us! We left everything behind, from personal effects to dog crates! Isn't that terrible?"

The lieutenant sighed.

"Listen, Emil. We did our duty, and we made our country proud. You, I, and the others were here for years, helping the Afghans build peace and democracy. The rest is up to them. It's up to them to maintain the progress we helped them make and build up their country."

"But..."

"That's enough!"

Emil opened his mouth to say something, but Brown elbowed him in the ribs.

"We should get there any moment," he said. "I wonder where we're going. I wouldn't mind Germany. I could do with a cold lager to wash off the dust in my throat. And a sausage."

"Couldn't we all? But I'd say Qatar is more likely. But they have beer too," the lieutenant said, and they all started talking about beer like they didn't have a care in the world, though they all stank of fear, shame, and hate.

That's humans for you. They say one thing when they mean another. I wonder if they ever fool anyone but themselves. We, dogs, don't do that. Maybe because we can't use words? Whether we growl, bark, or wag our tails, we always say precisely what we mean. That's why being a dog is so much easier!

The truck slowed to a crawl.

"There's the airport," someone said, and we all stuck our noses to the windows.

The place crawled with humans. Everywhere you looked, a sea of people: surrounding the trucks, scaling the walls, pushing against the gates to get in. Armed soldiers drove them away, but they didn't relent. Men clung to the trucks, trying to make it through the gates; veiled women offered their babies to soldiers to take them; kids cried, holding on to their mothers' skirts. The stench of fear and desperation was so foul that even the humans, who can't smell squat beyond beer, garlic, and bacon, clung to each other.

The guards pulled off the people who stuck to us like limpets and waved us through. The gates closed behind us, keeping out the crowd.

Our truck stopped amongst a thousand other trucks and cars, and the men sighed with relief and jumped out. Brown and I followed.

We filed up a dozen stairs, then down a grid walkway, the kind that lets you see what's below like you're walking on air — boy, do I hate those! — then into a room where a thousand people waited.

The soldiers sat on the floor, leaning against their packs. I lay on the cool concrete floor at Brown's feet, lapped the water he gave me, then curled for a nap.

"What's this dog doing here?"

A short man with tons of shiny bling on his chest glared at me down his long, thin nose.

"This is Rambo. He's an explosive-detecting K-9 working with our unit," Brown said.

Bling-man's mouth zipped into a line.

"Not anymore. This is not a minefield, sergeant; this is the freaking airport, and it's busy enough without people bringing their dogs here. Let me see his papers."

Brown handed him a bunch of papers.

"Are you kidding me? This dog is not even a military dog. He doesn't belong to the army! This is a contractor's dog. It needs to go!"

"Go where?"

"With the other dogs. We don't have enough capacity to fly out people, let alone dogs! Myers?"

"Sir?"

"Put this dog with the others."

Brown frowned.

"But how will he get home?"

"You'd better worry about how you'll get home, Sergeant. You and everyone else here. That's my primary responsibility. After every soldier gets home safely, we can start worrying about dogs. But for now..."

"But Sir, Rambo is not just a dog. He's a military K-9. He..."

"No, he's not. He's a contractor's dog. And even if he was military, he'd count as equipment. Do you have any idea how many millions of dollars of equipment we left behind? Helicopters, tanks, ammunition, dogs, and God knows what else. And you're gonna worry about a dog who doesn't even belong to the army? His owner will collect enough insurance to buy three new ones. Now, you all move."

He gestured to a door in the back, and the men collected their packs and filed toward it. All but Brown.

"But Sir, K-9 Rambo..."

Bling-man straightened to his whole five feet four and glared at Brown. He could barely reach Brown's chin, but he acted like the Alpha.

"Enough. Now go."

Brown opened his mouth, but the lieutenant grabbed his arm and pulled him to the door that had already swallowed the others.

"Brown, remember your career. And your family. You don't want to get in trouble."

"But Rambo..."

"Rambo will be fine. They'll look after him, and they'll fly him over as soon as they can. Now go."

I watched Brown open the door and step out. I tried to follow, but Myers held me back.

"Not you. You're not going."

"But..."

The door started closing. I leaped forward.

"Brown! Brown! You forgot me!" I barked.

But the door slammed shut.

## 37

Seriously?

I followed Myers through a narrow door, down a metal staircase to another gangplank. His boots echoed along the empty hallways. The whole place looked deserted, but I knew better. The ruckus of the crowd clawing their way in shook the walls, making the emptiness even more desolate.

I shivered.

Wherever Myers took me was not where I belonged. I belonged with Brown and the others, wherever they went. But once again, the humans didn't let me choose.

Myers opened the door to a metal stairway leading down three sets of stairs to a courtyard choking with crates. All full, by the sound and the smell.

The door behind us slammed shut with a bang, and the courtyard exploded into a cacophony of barks. Some low pitched, some high pitched, most in between. All asking to get out.

Myers shook his head.

"Briggs?"

"What?"

"I brought you another one."

"Great! Another mouth to feed. Just what I needed. How about some water and some kibble next time?"

Myers shrugged.

"Not my fault. The colonel told me to bring him here. Feel free to tell him no if you don't like it. Where do you want him?"

"Anywhere but here."

Briggs appeared from behind a pile of crates. He was thin, bald, and dirty, and he pressed a bloody tissue to his hand.

"What happened to you?"

"I got bit; that's what happened. By no less than a bloody chihuahua. I hate those ill-tempered yappy things. They're smaller than cats but harder to handle than Great Danes, for God's sake. Whenever there's trouble, you can bet they caused it. What have you got?"

"A bomb sniffer."

"A bomb sniffer? Really? They're gonna leave him here?"

"He apparently doesn't belong to the army. The colonel said he's just a contractor's dog."

"But still..."

"Listen, man, it's not my choice. As I said, feel free to bring it up with the colonel. Now, where do I put him?"

"There's a large empty crate in that corner. The Lab who was in it died last night. I didn't get to clean it, but it will have to do. And give him some water. This freaking sun is baking us here. You'd think they could have given us a shaded space, at least."

"Are you kidding? There isn't enough shade for the people. Hundreds of them are out there in the sun, waiting for a plane to take them somewhere, anywhere. And they're those who have papers, not the crowds outside. Your dogs are lucky to have this."

"They're not my dogs. I just look after them."

"Well, they surely aren't anyone else's. Go."

Myers sent me into the crate.

I sniffed it and pulled back. That was the filthiest crate I'd ever seen, smeared with someone else's blood and poop. It was terrible!

We, dogs, like poop as perfume. Even as an occasional snack, especially if it's frozen into poopsickles. But we don't poop in our crates. That's why they call it crate training. That's how we learn to stay clean.

But Myers didn't care. He pushed me in and slammed the door.

"See you later," he shouted.

"Did you give him water?"

The door slammed shut.

## 38

___

Now what?

I stuck my nose through the wire to find out who was there. It turned out that everyone was.

I'd never sniffed a more pathetic lot of dogs. Young and old, healthy and sick, big and small, the place is nothing but dogs stinking of misery and begging for release. They're so loud they cover the clamor of the crowds outside. To my left, to my right, and everywhere in between, there's nothing but hurting dogs.

My heart sinks.

When they figure out that Myers is gone, they start to settle. One by one, they lie down in their crates, panting to cope with the heat. The place gets quiet but for the hot breaths of a hundred dogs and their hopeless heartbeats. The silence feels even more desperate.

To my left, someone growls.

"Who are you?"

I sniff his way, but he's not familiar. I can't tell his breed, but I can feel his pain.

"I'm Rambo. I'm an explosive-detecting K-9 with the US Army. And you?"

"I'm Lucky."

Someone barks to my right, and, by the ear-piercing maniacal bark, I know it's got to be a chihuahua.

"The heck you are. You wouldn't be here if you were, you silly mutt."

Lucky growls.

"Mind your own business, Taco, or I'll show you a thing or two."

"You're locked in that crate. You can't show me nothing! Nothing! Nothing! Nothing!" Taco barks, setting everyone around him into a barking frenzy.

Lucky sighs.

"Ignore that lunatic. That Taco was no good to start with, and being locked in that crate drove him over the edge. That's why he bit Briggs. Moron! Figure that, biting the hand that feeds you. Only a chihuahua would do that."

"What's this place?" I ask.

"This is where they keep us until they can send us overseas. My human Judy said..."

Taco hollers.

"My human Judy, this, my human Judy, that. Is there anything else you can talk about?"

"You're just envious because your humans ditched you, and that's no wonder. Who'd want a hysterical little jerk like you? Not to mention that you're uglier than a cat."

"Yeah? And you're pretty? A mangy one-eared mutt off the streets of Kabul? I can't imagine what that Judy thought when she picked you up. She had to be blind."

"Judy picked me up because she's kind and generous. She picked up every stray dog and cat she could find and gave us all a good home. She taught us all to like and trust humans, even those of us who grew up in the streets."

"And great good did it do you. You'd be better off in the street, you stupid mutt! You'd be free, at least. But here? You're locked in a crate, and you can't even go scrounging for food. You'll just lie there baking in the sun until you die like Buddy did in that crate they put the new one in. What did you say your name was?"

"Rambo."

"Where the heck did you get a name like that?"

That gave me pause. Where the heck did I get a name like that?

"In Volendam. But that's not important right now. What are we doing here?"

"Like he said. Waiting for a plane to take us overseas. We might as well wait for snow. There aren't enough planes for humans and their stuff. We, dogs, aren't a priority. I've waited for days. That stupid street mutt has been here even longer. Still, we haven't seen anyone leave. Everyone's waiting. We jump up whenever that door opens, hoping they're here for us. But they never are. They just bring in another dog, like they brought you. Or take out the bodies. This place is like Hotel California. You can check-in anytime you like, but you can never leave."

He stops to scratch. I hope he's just nasty, but I somehow know he's right. This place is terrible. The stench of death, sickness, and despair turns my stomach. And I'm parched. Myers didn't give me any water, and the sun beats on my crate, making it hotter than the desert.

I pant and pant until my throat dries all the way to my stomach. I try to swallow, but I have no more drool, and my tongue sticks to the roof of my mouth. So I force myself to ignore the dirt and the blood and lie down to soak in some chill from the ground. But this ground has no chill.

Far away, someone screams.

"Let me out! Let me out!"

It's like a signal. Everyone joins in. Hundreds of voices, hoarse from thirst and screaming, call out their fear, loneliness, and sorrow. Taco chimes in, and Lucky follows. It takes all I've got to stay quiet. I know it won't do me any good; it will just parch my throat even further.

A bell rings, and the howls turn into a barking frenzy. Crate doors open and close, and the smell of kibble drifts in.

"Dinner! Dinner!" Taco yaps. Lucky follows.

I'm not hungry, but I'm so thirsty I could drink a river. So, when my door opens, and Briggs brings water, I lap it in seconds.

Briggs shakes his head.

"That Myers. He didn't give you any water, did he? What a tool!"

He refills my bowl, and I'm grateful, though being grateful is the last thing on my mind. What I am — besides being hot, thirsty, and lonely — is angry. I've never, ever been so mad.

## 39

Anger doesn't come easy to me. I've never been out of control. Not even when that scorpion bit me in Angola. Or when those strays cornered me in the Punji stick pit. I'm just an easygoing kind of guy. So I wonder where this rage comes from?

It must have started when Myers locked me in without water.

But no. It started when the door slammed shut, and Brown left me behind without looking back.

Not even. It started when I ate the key to the supply room to leave Prozac something to drink. I'm still struggling to get rid of it. I didn't know if Prozac was even alive, but I couldn't wrap my mind around abandoning him instead of doing whatever it took to get him back.

Nope. It was before that when Lovely lost her nose, and they sent her away. I still wonder if they put her down.

Even before that, at Viper's retirement party. They hung that ugly tag around his neck and threw him out of the army, the only home he knew. If I live to be a hundred, I'll never forget his heartbreaking smell of despair. He didn't care for me, but his memory tears at my heart.

I choke.

Lucky sniffs my sorrow.

"You OK, Rambo?"

"Sure."

But I'm anything but. I'm heartbroken and burning with rage.

Then it dawns on me.

I don't think humans care about us dogs. They always abandon us when we're no longer useful. Like now.

I listen to the cries of a hundred inmates, and I wonder what's next. Will they really fly us away? Or will they leave us here to die from heat and thirst?

Lucky smells my thoughts.

"It's gonna be OK, you'll see. They'll come for us. I know it."

Taco chokes with laughter.

"You stupid mutt! You'd think growing up in the streets would've taught you better! They say that only the smart ones survive, but you're a living example that's not true. How could you stay alive when you're so stupid?"

"Shut up, Taco. I know Judy will come for me."

"Of course. And the world is a place of love and beauty, storks bring children, and Santa comes with gifts every winter."

Taco laughed so hard his crate rattled.

"Even New Boy here knows better, and he's only been here half a day. You, I, and all the other pathetic mutts in this wretched place will die here. The humans abandoned us, and we'll roast to death in these filthy crates. We'll all die waiting."

But we didn't. Not the three of us, at least.

Day after day went by, and Briggs kept us alive. He brought us food and water, cursed every time he found someone dead, and swore every time Myers brought him a new inmate to look after. But he kept going.

But one day the metal door opened, and Myers shouted from the door

"Come on, Briggs. We're leaving."

"Leaving? Where?"

"Back home. The Taliban are at the gates, about to take over. The last plane is on the runway, warming its engines. Let's go!"

"But…"

"But what?"

"But the dogs?"

"Are you insane? The Taliban are here, and you're worried about a pack of mutts? Come on! Let's go!"

"But they'll die with no water and no food!"

"Don't you worry, they won't suffer long. You know how the Taliban like dogs. I bet they'll shoot every single one right there in their crates. Let's go!"

"I can't leave the dogs here like that!"

"Are you stupid or what? Didn't you hear me? This is the last plane. The Taliban will shoot the dogs whether you're here or not. As for you? They'll parade you in the streets for everyone to see, torture you and kill you on live TV. How would you like your parents to see you burn alive? Come on, Briggs! You know you can't stay here!"

"But I can't leave the dogs like this!"

"Suit yourself."

The metal door slammed shut, but the dogs' screams covered its noise. Everyone barked, yelled, shrieked, and scratched their way out in a racket so loud it covered the one outside.

The terror of a hundred dogs filled my nose. They'd all heard Myers, and they knew what was coming. Old dogs barked their anger, puppies cried their fear, and everyone screamed their loneliness.

My heart sank. We'll all die alone. This filthy crate is the last thing I'll see, and the stench of terror is the last thing I'll ever smell.

First, I froze with fear. Then I got mad.

I curled down in my crate and breathed, trying to ignore the stench. To take my mind off my death, I wondered how my friends had died.

I hoped Frieda's death was peaceful and painless. The old girl deserved it. But, as always, thinking of Frieda fills me with remorse.

If only I hadn't left camp that night...

But the guilt chokes me even worse than my fear. To take my mind off it, I wonder what happened to Prozac, Lovely, and Viper. Are they dead or alive? Either way, I hope they're better off than I am. Thinking of them makes me sad, but not guilty. I did all I could for each of them.

But Cersei...

Somewhere, at the other end of the world, Cersei's white eyes look down the dusty driveway, watching for my return. Her ears perk up to listen for Mike's truck, and she sniffs the wind to smell me. She wakes up every morning hoping today's the day I return. She goes to bed every night hoping I'll come back tomorrow.

But I won't. Not today, not tomorrow, not ever.

I'll die right here in this filthy crate.

I was still lying with my nose on my paws, feeling sorry for myself, when a crate door screeched open. Then another.

Lucky barked with excitement.

"I'm out! I'm out!"

His face shining with sweat, Briggs opened my door, then moved on to Taco. When he finished opening the crates, he split open two bags of kibble. He let them spill on the ground, then ran up the steps and let the heavy door slam shut behind him.

A black-and-white spotted dog missing half his left ear wagged his skinny tail and barked:

"We're free! We're free!"

That's got to be Lucky, I thought. I wagged my tail to greet him, but a bat-faced scrawny chihuahua beat me to him. Taco, I bet.

"The hell we are. See those?"

Shiny metal walls taller than I could ever hope to scale reflected the sun over dozens of crates crammed in a space no bigger than our barracks. There was no shade other than under the two skinny shelves in the corner, loaded with water jugs and bags of kibble. And no door other than the one Briggs flew through, two floors up those nasty grid steps making you feel like you're stepping on air.

Taco was right. There was no way out.

I turned back to Lucky, but he was locked in a stand-off with four other dogs who rushed to claim the kibble, growling at each other with their mouths full.

But most dogs stayed in their crates. They stuck their noses through the doors to see what happened, but they didn't dare come out.

Good for them, I thought. This doesn't smell good.

Sure enough, just heartbeats later, the kibble ran out, and the fight started. Heart-chilling growls turned into snarls. A black dog barked; a white one screamed, then ran with his tail between his legs when Lucky's teeth sank into his shoulder. The scent of blood filled the air, bringing me back to that Khmer pit, and I got dizzy with anger.

The humans abandoned us again. They left us to ourselves with no way out. We were just as trapped as in our crates but no longer safe from each other.

The small dogs cowered in their crates as the big dogs fought over the last of the kibble. When it was all gone, Lucky returned, licking his shoulder and wagging his tail like a flag.

"That was fun! I haven't had a good fight ever since I moved in with Judy. I was worried I'd lost my touch, but no. It's just like swimming — once you learn, you never forget it."

Taco glared at him.

"Look at you, all scratched and bitten! Mom was right: You can take the mutt off the street, but you can't take the street out of the mutt."

Lucky cocked his head.

"What?"

"No matter how long you live — and the way you're going, it won't be long — you'll always be a street mutt. There's just no cleaning that out of you."

"Of course not. That's who I am. I'm a seventh-generation free dog and proud of it. Unlike you, whose parents and grandparents lived off the humans' hand-me-downs, we made it on our own. My mom, her mom, and her mom's mom lived long enough to bring up pups not by licking human hands but by being shrewd and smart."

"You've got to take after your dad then."

"Maybe? I bet he was no slouch if he could woo my mom."

"So how come you went to live with Judy? If your folks were too proud to eat the humans' hand-me-downs, how come you left the street to stay with her?"

"Judy saved my life. She took me in when I got hit by a car and I was too weak to look for food. She nursed me back to health. After that, I stayed with her not for the food but for love. The food was secondary. And it wasn't that great either. Just kibble, and I hate kibble. Gimme a juicy bone any day...."

"You and your food. Look up, stupid."

He wasn't talking to me, but I looked up anyhow.

The metal door had opened, and three bearded men in shalwar kameez pointed their guns at us.

## 41

The Taliban stared at us like we had three ears.

"What the heck? What are those dogs doing here?"

The tall one lowered his gun and stepped forward to see better. The short one behind him scratched his head.

"Maybe the infidels keep them for food like we keep our goats? You know they'll eat anything, even pigs."

The third man scratched his gray beard and laughed.

"You're a stupid country boy, Faiz! Americans don't eat dogs. They use them to find explosives. And hunt us."

Faiz shook his head and pointed at Taco.

"Look at that one, Abdul. That can't be a working dog! And that mutt over there! And the other!"

The first man shrugged.

"Who cares what they're here for? What matters is that we found nothing useful: no weapons, no ammunition, no equipment. Nothing. Let's keep searching before the others get it all."

"What should we do with the dogs? Should we kill them?" Faiz asked.

"Why waste precious time and ammunition for a pack of filthy dogs? Without food and water, they'll die anyhow. Let's go."

He headed to the door, but Abdul stayed put, staring at me.

"See that one there? The striped one with sharp ears? I've seen one just like that in our village. The Americans had it look for explosives and weapons. I bet that's one of those bomb sniffers."

Faiz lifted his gun.

"You want me to shoot him, Abdul? I'm a good shot; I can do it from right here; I don't even need to go down the stairs. Want me to show you?"

He lifted his weapon, but Abdul slammed down his hand.

"Calm down, will you? If I wanted him shot, I could shoot him myself."

Faiz shrugged.

"So, what do you want then?"

"I wonder if we could use him."

"Use him? For what?"

"For whatever the infidels trained him for. To find explosives, weapons, and ammunition. For us."

Faiz stared at him like he hung the moon.

"You're so wise, Abdul. I wish I had a quarter of your wisdom. You're right; let's use him. But...how do we do that?"

"We'll figure it out later. For now, you, Faiz, stay here to look after the dogs. They're ours. Don't let anyone touch them, but give them some water. And food. Ismail and I will be back later."

"But Abdul..."

"What?"

"How about the stuff? You said we'll get weapons and ammunition. You even said I could keep the first pair of goggles. I won't get nothing if I just stay here to watch these filthy dogs."

"Don't worry, Faiz. Ismail and I will share everything we find. But you have to take good care of them. Don't let anyone touch them, don't let them kill each other, and don't let them escape."

Abdul left. Ismail followed. Faiz took two steps to follow them, but he stopped at the door and looked back. He glanced after his friends, then scowled at us.

He's like three floors away, but I can smell from down here that he's not happy. He'd much rather shoot us than look after us.

No wonder. The whole pack barks, growls, yaps, and screams, loud enough to shake the walls. They don't care if the humans are American, Afghans, or Khmers. All they care about is water and kibble.

Faiz shouts something, but his voice drowns in the ruckus. He screams again, but to no avail.

He shakes his head and heads down the stairs, holding his gun ready to shoot. He takes one careful step after another.

"Get back, you filthy mutts."

The dogs back up. Even those who don't know what guns are know that sticks and rocks hurt.

Faiz glances at the food and water jugs on the shelves. He slides sideways, holding his back against the wall and his gun pointed at the mob until he gets close.

Then he turns and shoots the bags.

It's like a bomb exploded. The small metal yard turns to chaos. The dogs cower, the bullets ricochet, raising dust. Someone yelps, someone else screams, and the kibble rains over the yard like hail. They all rush to get some, and the ruckus of growls, snarls, and barks shakes the walls.

Faiz freezes, staring at the chaos.

It's time.

I take off like a rocket. I don't look down at the darn metal grid that makes you feel like you're walking on air. I don't look back either. I only look at the open door at the top of the stairs.

One more landing and...

A bullet hits the step under my paw. Another one grazes my shoulder and slams the door as I fly through it like the wind.

**42**

I run for my life like I know where I'm going. But I don't. I just take any open door I can find in this metal maze, so empty that my steps echo like there are a dozen running dogs, not just me.

I slow down to reorient.

The empty hallway I'm on goes as far as I can see. Right and left, metal doors gape open to rooms full of stuff: boxes, canisters, containers. More stuff's scattered all over the floors: backpacks, helmets, broken goggles, a lone glove.

They left in a hurry. But where did they go?

I get sniffing, and a familiar scent hits my nose. Really?

I sniff again to make sure.

Yep. That's Briggs. He was here just minutes ago. Did he catch that last flight?

Only one way to find out.

I track his scent along the corridor, down a set of stairs into another hallway, then up another set of stairs.

Humans! They complicate everything. Still, it's way easier than the agility course Mike trained me on, so I move on.

Briggs's scent gets stronger. He was here just moments ago.

What on earth took him so long? I know he runs on his hind paws, like all humans, but still.

I turn the corner and find out.

There's Briggs, limping down the hallway, leaning on his weapon. He smells like pain, and his bald head shines with sweat as he mumbles something under his breath.

I greet him with a tail wag, and his eyes grow wide.

"Rambo? How on earth did you get here, pal?"

I cock my head.

"I managed. But what happened to you? And where's that darn plane?"

"I misstepped and sprained my ankle, so I barely hobbled here. I don't even know if they're still here."

"Just one way to find out. Let's go!"

I go ahead to encourage him, but he's Dog-awful slow.

I run circles around him to get him moving, but it takes him forever to climb a set of stairs. Then he stops to breathe.

"Come on, Briggs. We're almost there. Just one more...."

Steps echo behind us, along the hallway we just left.

"Darn it! They're coming."

Briggs bites his lip and stumbles forward, but he's awful slow. The steps get closer and closer. No way can he get out of here before they come. I could run ahead, of course. But I can't leave him behind. Darn!

"You keep going. I'll be back," I growl.

I rush back down the stairs, hook a left, and start barking like I saw a cat.

The steps stop and change direction, coming for me now. I need to hide.

I find a pile of boxes in a corner, squeeze behind them, and hold my breath.

I see three pairs of boots taking one cautious step after another. Three shalwar kameez, then three bearded men come into sight, holding on to their weapons.

They look up and down the corridor.

"Where did he go?"

"He can't be far. You two go that way; I'll go the other," the oldest one gestures.

I watch them creep down the hallway and wait until they're out of sight before I climb back upstairs to Briggs.

But Briggs is gone.

**43**

———————

What the heck?

I track him through one door, then another. How did he move so fast when he could barely hobble?

I find out when I turn the corner. Two soldiers drag Briggs through the last door to the runway, where the last plane roars.

I run to Briggs.

"Nice job! We caught it!"

Briggs smiles.

"Good job, Rambo. Thank you!"

The soldiers frown.

"What the heck? What's this dog doing here?"

"He's with me," Briggs says.

They shake their heads.

"The colonel won't like it. He said we don't have enough room for people. There's no way he'll take any dogs," they say, helping Briggs through the plane's door.

"He's the last one."

The guard nods.

"High time. But what's with the dog?"

"He's with me," Briggs says.

The guard shakes his head.

"I can't let him in. The colonel said nothing about dogs on this plane. Sorry."

"I'm not going without him."

The guard shrugs.

"Sorry."

He pulls the door closed, but Briggs sticks his foot in the door and pushes it open. The guard stares at him like he's nuts.

"You can't stay behind. You know damn well what will happen if you do."

Briggs hobbles out.

"Enough already! Just let in that darn dog, and let's get going before they shoot us down," Myers says.

The door slams shut behind me.

**44**

———

I curled at Briggs' feet with my nose under my tail. That always helps me sleep, since it keeps intruding smells on low. Every once in a while, I opened an eye to check on things, but nothing happened. The men sat packed like sardines, their shoulders touching, but nobody said a word until the pressure in my ears made me yawn.

"We'll be landing soon," someone said.

"Landing where?" Briggs asked.

"Qatar, I think. What difference does it make? Wherever it is, it won't be home."

A pimply kid pushed his helmet off his eyes.

"It can't be any worse than Kandahar."

The others laughed with no joy.

"What's with your helmet, kid? Did you steal your father's?"

The kid shrugged.

"I must have switched it. Someone, somewhere, wears my helmet on top of his head like an ornament. Either way, I'm glad to be out."

Silence.

"Aren't you?"

"What?"

"Glad to be out?"

"Yeah. But not like that, with our tails between our legs, leaving everything behind," Briggs said.

"What did you leave behind?"

"Not me. We. We left behind thousands of people desperate to get out for fear the Taliban will kill them, and hundreds of dogs they'll slaughter. Unless they die from thirst."

Briggs's anger turns his sweat rancid.

"How did you manage to save this one?"

"I didn't. I left him to die with the others. But he escaped and saved me."

Briggs's clammy hands rub my ears. He's not a bad guy, Briggs, and he tried. I lick his hand, where Taco's bite hasn't healed yet, and he sighs.

"I wonder what happened to the others."

"Better wonder what happens to this one," a chunky man says. "You know they'll lock him up when we arrive?"

"Lock him up? Why?"

"Rabies is endemic in Afghanistan, so they won't let him back in the states. He'll have to quarantine for months before going anywhere. You have his papers?"

"What papers?"

"His ID, his vaccination records, and whatever else. You got them?"

"I have nothing."

"That's bad, man. You can't just smuggle dogs from the Middle East and take them to the States! Take some pictures, at least, if you want to have a prayer of ever finding him again."

When we land, two men in protective gear lock me in a crate and take me away.

"Don't worry, Rambo, I'll get you home," Briggs says.

But I don't believe him. And I can smell he doesn't believe it either.

And home? What home?

## 45

My new kennel was white and clean and smelled like bleach. It wasn't hot, it wasn't cold, it wasn't cramped, and I even had a patch of dirt.

But it was boring.

Kibble in the morning, kibble at night. Other than that, nothing to do but clean my privates and lie with my nose on my paws.

Every once in a while, I'd hear a bark, a door, or a car. But I never got to see them. They called it isolation. I called it the most boring time of my life.

It got so bad that I almost wished I'd stayed with Lucky and Taco. I wondered if the Taliban taught them how to sniff for explosives, they shot them, or let them die of thirst.

I never heard from Briggs again, but I didn't expect to. It took me a while, but I finally learned that humans always abandon the dogs they don't need.

With nothing better to do, I chewed on my bowl, cleaned my tail, and thought about my friends. To keep busy, I made up stories about what happened to them.

First, Arco, my puppyhood friend. He's got to be five now like I am. It's been years since he trained for protection. I bet he lives the good life somewhere, eats grass-fed gourmet organic food, and pees on well-kept lawns as he watches his hot-shot human play golf.

As for Lovely, the spirited springer, I must admit I had a crush on her. And no wonder. That girl was dynamite. She had dazzling red ears, a sexy tail, and the best nose in the business. I didn't try to hit on her because I didn't want to hurt Viper's feelings. Then she lost her nose and disappeared. But I can almost see her strutting her stuff on the runway, competing for The Best in Show.

Then Viper, the veteran. He served his whole life, then the army sent him to a family he dreaded just to get rid of him. But I bet Viper whipped them into shape. Somewhere in America, the best-trained family belongs to Viper.

Old Prozac disappeared in the mountains. The Taliban took him and Cho, and we never heard from them again. Prozac wasn't young, and those mountains were harsh. And so are the Taliban. Did they force him to work for them, or did he manage to escape through the mountains?

Common sense tells me Zak is gone, but I can't take that. I'm miserable enough already. So I make up a story where Prozac gets to escape, he crosses the mountains, finds our trucks, and goes back to business. I can see him sitting by the driver, his eyes glued to the road and his floppy ears floating in the breeze.

Oh, Zak, how I miss you!

The only one I can't think about is Cersei. She was already old and blind when I left.

It just hurts too much.

**46**

———————

Then, one morning, they let me out.

I knew it was morning because I'd just had breakfast. It was the same as every other morning, but the air smelled different.

They loaded me in a truck. Then a plane. Then another car.

By the time I finally stopped, I no longer knew if it was today, yesterday, or tomorrow. I just knew I was far away.

I shook my head to clear up the fog when he opened my crate.

"How're you doing, old boy?"

He'd shrunk since I last saw him. But his smell hadn't changed, nor the touch of his hands on my ears.

"Good to see you, Rambo."

He let me out. I struggled to my paws, then wobbled to bless the spring-smelling bushes. I sniffed the air, and the scent of rich mud filled my heart. Now we're talking! I looked for a puddle.

"Rambo?"

The earth shifted.

"Is that you?"

An orange dog in a shaggy coat too big for her stands in the doorway. Her legs shake, but she holds her head high to sniff my way, watching me with white eyes. She's old and frail, but she's still here.

My heart melts.

"Cersei?"

"It is you!"

She steps forward, and I rush to meet her before she tumbles down the stairs. I offer her my butt, and she sniffs it; then I check hers. We lick each other's noses.

"It's good to have you back, kid."

"So good to see you, Cersei. I..."

Something jumps me.

"I told you he was coming," Tyrion purrs, rubbing his furry face against mine. "You didn't believe me, but I knew."

Cersei snorts.

"You and your nine lives. You stupid cats think everyone lives forever."

"I'm not stupid. And I'm not a cat," Tyrion hisses.

"No? What are you then?"

"I'm a Farking F-Line. That's what Mike said just yesterday when I dropped that dead rat in his bed."

"If you think that's a compliment..."

A truck stops in the driveway. Butch jumps out.

"I'd be darned! I can't believe it! You really got him back! How on earth did you do it?"

"It wasn't just me. It was teamwork. The soldier who smuggled him out posted his picture and found his last handler. He got in touch with someone named Ash, who crowdfunded to get him flown back."

"Good for you. But I can't take him back. I already collected his insurance, and it's enough to get three brand new dogs instead of a middle-aged mutt."

"I wouldn't let you have him if you wanted him. He's mine."

Cersei growls. "I don't think so. Look at what you did to him. He's mine."

Tyrion rubs himself around my legs. "Are you all nuts? Rambo's mine."

I look from one to the other and I wag my tail. "I don't think so. You all are mine."

---

## 47

Life was good on the farm. Instead of sniffing for explosives, I learned to herd cattle and check fences. Mike and I went around the ranch every day, leaving Tyrion to look after Cersei.

Tyrion didn't like it.

He hissed and got himself fluffed up like a toilet brush, then stared at me with his otherworldly green eyes.

"Why do I have to look after that old bitch?"

"Would you rather look after Mike, count cows, and mend fences?"

"Cows stink!"

"I beg to differ. Nothing smells better — other than dead fish and bacon. But that's not the point. I can't be both at home and on the ranch. Which would you rather do?"

"Neither. I'd rather chase squirrels and nap in the sun."

"You can do that after I get home. I'll look after Mike and Cersei, and you can go have fun."

Tyrion's eyes opened wide.

"When do you have fun?"

I cocked my head. When do I have fun? What does having fun even mean?

"Not your problem. We have a deal?"

Tyrion shifted his weight from his right paw to his left in a cat dance, then rubbed around my legs like he always does when he wants to soften me, but that didn't work. I have to look after Mike and Cersei — and Tyrion, of course — but I can't do it all.

"Darn. I'll look after her while you're gone. But then she's all yours."

"Of course."

That's why Tyrion was chasing something somewhere the afternoon the doorbell rang.

Cersei barked up a storm like she always does. Not seeing things made it essential for her to point them out to those who do.

Mike took off to answer and locked me in the bathroom, where I supervised him do his business.

"Yes?"

"Would you happen to have a K-9 named Rambo?"

Mike took in a deep breath.

"Who wants to know?"

"I'm Ashley. I worked with Rambo in Kandahar. And Cambodia."

"Come in then."

The bathroom door opened.

"Rambo? You have guests."

I rushed to greet her, but something told me I shouldn't jump on her, so I just sniffed her all over and licked her hands. They smelled like lavender, as always, but her leg smelled like metal, and she leaned on a cane.

"Ash! It's you! I can't believe it! How are you?"

Her thin hands rubbed my ears.

"Boy, am I glad to see you. How are you, Rambo?"

I wagged my tail.

"Not bad. How are you?"

"Better now that I found you."

She pushed her blonde hair from her tired blue eyes and smiled, but I could smell she was hurting. Mike sensed it too.

"Have a seat. How about a drink?"

"No drink, thanks. I have a long drive back. But I'll take a seat. Rambo and I go way back. He saved my life, you know. That day I got wounded in Kandahar, I would have bled to death if Rambo hadn't been there to get my tourniquet. I couldn't settle before I knew how he was. I'd be glad to take him off your hands anytime."

Mike laughed.

"I don't think so. Rambo's the best thing that happened to me in forever. My ex used to say that I cared more about him than I did for the kids. No way will I let him go."

Ash laughed.

"Doesn't that sound familiar! Not the kids, but the rest."

Mike sighed. "Isn't that odd? Like it's either them or the dogs. But it's not either/or. It's both. Dogs make everything better."

"Yep. It's been hard since I lost my leg, and I haven't been able to walk well enough to look after a dog."

"You lost your leg?"

"A grenade in Kandahar. My knee got shattered, and they couldn't save it. But I got a prosthesis."

Mike smiled. "Tell me about it."

He lifted his pants to show his gleaming metal ankles. Ashley's eyes widened.

"Wow! Two?"

"You'll get used to it; you'll see. And you'll ditch that cane in no time. How about that drink, though? I have an extra bedroom and a dog who'll look after you."

Ash smiled. "Don't mind if I do."


Next in series: **K-9 PROZAK: POW**

First in series: **BECOMING K-9: A Bomb Dog's Memoir**

# AFTERWORD

Thanks for reading K-9 Rambo. I hope you enjoyed it. If you did, please **take a minute to leave a review**, and tell a friend. That will help others find this book, and I'd appreciate it.

If you haven't already, check out the other books in the **K-9 HEROES series: BECOMING K-9, BIONIC BUTTER, K-9 VIPER, LOVELY K-9 and K-9 PROZAC.**

Go to **RadaJones.com** to sign up for updates, get freebies and stay in touch. I love hearing from you!

Rada

# ABOUT THIS BOOK

Rambo's memoir is a work of fiction. Other than Peemail, dogs don't write much, and they publish even less. They can read our souls, but their spelling is nothing to write home about.

Speaking dog is not about rolling your tongue to make silly sounds; it's about watching, listening, and feeling each other in your hearts. That's why dogs don't lie. How can you lie when you taste someone's tears, breathe in their soul and listen to their heartbeat? There's no room for deception in Dog like in human language.

This book is a love letter to Rambo and the other dogs who make our world a better place. May we deserve them.

Rada

## ABOUT THE AUTHOR

Rada was born in Transylvania, ten miles from Dracula's Castle. Growing up between communists and vampires taught her that humans are fickle, but you can always trust dogs and books. That's why she read every book she could get, including the phone book (too many characters, not enough action), and adopted every stray she found, from dogs to frogs.

After joining her American husband, she spent years studying medicine and working in the ER, but she still speaks like Dracula's cousin.

Rada, her husband Steve, and their dog Guinness live in a cozy Adirondack cabin ruled by a deaf black cat named Paxil. They spend their days writing, hiking, and dreaming about traveling to faraway places.

Go to RadaJones.com to sign up for updates and freebies.

facebook.com/RadaJonesMD

twitter.com/JonesRada

instagram.com/RadaJonesMD

bookbub.com/profile/rada-jones

# BOOKS BY RADA JONES

**BECOMING K-9:** A Bomb Dog's Memoir

**BIONIC BUTTER:** A Three-Pawed K-9 Hero

**K-9 VIPER:** The Veteran's Story

**LOVELY K-9:** A Prison Puppy

**K-9 RAMBO:** The Dutch Master

**K-9 PROZAK:** POW

**OVERDOSE:** An ER Phycological Thriller

(ER Crimes: The Steele Files Book 1)

**MERCY:** An ER Thriller

(ER Crimes: The Steele Files Book 2)

**POISON:** An ER Thriller

(ER Crimes: The Steele Files Book 3)

**STAY AWAY FROM MY ER,** and Other Fun Bits of Wisdom

**ER CRIMES:** The Steele Files

Box Set: Books 1-3

# EXCERPT FROM K-9 PROZAK

POW

I peek inside the cave, but the harsh sun has burned my eyes, and all I see is darkness. No light, no movement, no sound. Nothing but the stench of hate and the taste of impending doom.

I sit and point my nose to the cave to warn Cho, my handler. But she's not watching me. She's crawling up the massive boulder that blocks the trail. I struggled with it too. Made me wonder if it got there on purpose.

Far below, the men pant and curse as they stumble up the steep goat path, bent by their heavy equipment. Those military boots may be great in the desert, but here, where bare rock gives way to rolling gravel and treacherous stones that shift under your weight, boots are stiff and clumsy. Thank Dog, I have paws.

I watch them struggle to come up, and my heart sinks. From the top of my nose to the tip of my tail, I know that something's wrong; I just don't know what.

I sniff again.

None of the scents I'm trained to look for - no plastics, TNT, or black powder. But I know something's off.

I stare at Cho, willing her to stop, but she's not paying attention to me. She looks at her feet to plan her next step.

That's not new. Ever since we met, Cho's always been in her bubble.

I'd been with law enforcement and border patrol for most of my life. But when things heated up in Afghanistan, they sent me here to sniff for IEDs. That's when I met Cho. She was young and worried and too small for her uniform. And she hated touching me.

That was weird because, from toddlers to retirees, everyone tries to pet me. It goes with being a charming golden retriever that no one can resist. I sometimes wish they'd keep their hands to themselves. But, for the most part, I love belly rubs and tail scratches. You can never have too many.

But Cho's cautious eyes and forbidding smell told me she didn't want me anywhere near her. So I stayed put when the lieutenant introduced us.

"Cho, this is Prozak. He's been with the Border Patrol and Law Enforcement. He can find anything you want, from bananas to bombs. And he's a good boy with an excellent disposition. If you lived to a hundred, you'd never find a better K-9. You're very fortunate to have him, you know? Take good care of him."

He scratched my ears and glanced at Cho under furrowed eyebrows. I could smell he didn't like her, though I didn't know why. But humans are like that. There's seldom any rhyme or reason to what they do, so I chalked it up to human weirdness.

That's how we got started, months ago. I hoped things would get better between us, but they didn't. Cho never touches me unless she needs to, and she always smells like she's expecting some disaster.

So I gave her space, though it wasn't easy. Ever since Ruby, humans have been an essential part of my life. Bonding with them makes me whole. But Cho isn't into bonding.

I wonder what she's into. She doesn't like being here, but then nobody does. She doesn't like the men. She doesn't even like Ash, Rambo's handler, the only other female in camp who's a sweetheart. And she surely doesn't like touching me.

But that's not important right now. What's important is that I warn the men that something's wrong. I bark to tell Cho, but she pretends she doesn't hear me.

Oh well. One's got to do what one's got to do.

I raise my muzzle to the sky and sing the song of my people. I howl like I haven't howled since the day I found Ruby.

My howl bounces from peak to peak, building into a chorus. It's like there's a dozen howling Prozaks, not just me.

Another howl answers.

Is it the echo?

No. It's Rambo, telling me he's got it.

I sigh with relief.

I know he'll do his best to keep them safe: Ash, Emil, Brown, Pimply Dan, even the lieutenant. I'll do my best to keep Cho safe.

She's finally made it over that boulder. Her chest heaving, she stops to look around and listen.

There's nothing but the silence and these mountains baring their ugly fangs. We are alone.

She takes out a vial and breaks it over a piece of cloth. Then, for the first time ever, she touches me without needing to. She grabs my collar and covers my mouth and nose with that stinky wet cloth.

I try to shake it off, but I can't. She holds me tight.

I breathe the fumes and my brain fogs.

I know this is poison, so I struggle to escape, but my legs go weak, and I drop to the ground.

The world turns black.

~

**Buy K-9 PROZAK**

# EXCERPT FROM BECOMING K-9

A BOMB DOG'S MEMOIR

Who knew training humans was so hard? You'd wonder why. They aren't that stupid. It takes them a while, but they eventually learn when you want out, you're hungry or you're thirsty. They can even talk to each other by making noise with their tongue. How weird is that? Even my brother Blue, who's the slowest of us all, knows that the tongue is for lapping water and panting to cool down.

Mom cocked her head and licked my nose.

"That's the best they can do, dear. They have no tails, their ears don't move, and most don't even have enough fur to raise their hackles. No wonder they're confused and need us to guide them. And that's what we do; that's our life's work. But we need to choose them carefully."

Mom was on her sixth litter and very wise. Beautiful, too, with her long muzzle, amber eyes, and smooth, shiny fur, all black but for her golden legs and loving pink tongue.

She glanced at Yellow, who chased his tail instead of paying attention, and growled. He hung his head and sat in line with the rest of us to listen.

It was a lovely summer day as Mom homeschooled us in Jones's front yard. The warm wind tickled my nose. I bit it, but I caught nothing. I tried again, but Mother threw me a side glance, so I closed my mouth and sat still.

"Boys and girls, today's the day. People will come to check you out and choose which one to take home. They don't know it, but it doesn't work that way. You choose your humans, but choose them wisely. Sniff them all, then pick the ones that smell like food if you want a good life. You may sometimes get bacon, maybe even grapes. Humans say dogs don't eat grapes, but that's poppycock. They just want to keep them for themselves. My grandma was a pure-bred Alsatian, and she loved Riesling. I never had Riesling, but Concord isn't bad."

A shiny strip of drool dripped from Mom's mouth. She licked it off and inspected us. We were seven: three boys and four girls. But that doesn't much matter when you're just ten weeks old. The only difference is how you pee. The boys don't know how to squat so they need something to lift their leg to, like a bush or a mailbox. How stupid!

"Why don't you just lift your leg, if that's what you need to do? What does the bush have to do with anything?"

"Leave them alone, Red."

I tried, but it was hard. I was the runt of the litter, so I had to prove myself all the time. Mom said I had a Napoleonic complex.

"What's that?"

"It's when you're the smallest, so you have to be meaner to show them that size doesn't matter."

I told you Mom is brilliant. She came all the way from Germany when she was just a pup. Our human, Jones, has two passions: German shepherds and history. Mom was his first German shepherd, and he spent lots of time teaching her things most dogs never heard about.

He still does, even now that she's old. He sits in his recliner and reads to her as she lays by the fireplace. Sometimes I listen in. There was a story about a dude named Hitler. Not a nice guy, but for loving German shepherds. Another one about that short guy

Napoleon who tried to conquer the world while wearing funny hats. And one about some place called Afghanistan.

"That's a bad war, Maddie," Jones said, scratching the four white hairs in his beard. "Those Taliban, they are not nice people."

He calls her Maddie, but her real name is Madeline Rose Kahn Van Jones. He is Jones. The Van is for Van Gogh, some orange dude who got so mad he bit off his own ear. The rest is just for show, since people pay more for dogs with long names; they call that a pedigree. Mom's pedigree is longer than her tail.

As always, Mom was right. People came to see us, and they brought their spouses, their kids, and even their dogs to check us out and choose which one to get. Like, really? Jones said that only one out of twenty German shepherd owners is smarter than his dog. I don't believe it. I bet he fudged the numbers to feel better. You think you own a dog? Who feeds who? Who cleans after who? Who does the work, everything but making decisions? You, human, in case you didn't know it. You don't buy a dog; you hire supervision. But I digress.

My littermates and I wore colored collars so humans could tell us apart. There was no need, really, since we were all different, but humans couldn't see it. What color did I wear? Red, of course. I was small, but I was the queen of the litter, whether the others liked it or not.

A fat man in a Hawaiian shirt stopped to stare at me. He called his female.

"Look at this red one! Isn't he cute?"

She hobbled closer, leaning on her crooked stick. I love sticks, so I tried to take it. She didn't want to let go, but I insisted. They laughed.

"Let's get him."

Jones cleared his throat.

"Red is lovely, indeed, but she's a very active little person who needs a lot of attention. How much time do you plan to work with her every day?"

"Work with her?"

"Yes. Walk her, train her, and play with her."

They stared at him like he'd lost his marbles. He smiled.

"May I recommend Brown here? He's lovely, easygoing, and eager to please. He'll be happy to lay on the sofa watching TV. Or Miss Green? She's a polite little lady who gets along with everyone and never disappoints."

Brown left. So did Green, Yellow, and even White, while I stayed, waiting for my forever home.

"Take it easy, Red dear," Mother said when there were only two of us left—Black and me. "You need to soften up a bit; otherwise, you'll be left without a family. People look for easygoing dogs to fit into their lives, not for somebody to take charge. Though maybe they should, really, but they aren't smart enough to know that."

Her German accent made her words feel harsh. Have you ever listened to Germans? It's like they're constipated while they also have a cold. They keep clearing their throats, so their words come out like bullets from a machine gun. I don't speak German, but I love watching old war movies with Jones.

"What do you mean, Mom? What should I do?"

"Lick their hands, sweetheart. Wrap yourself around their feet and stare at them like they hung the moon."

"Are you serious?"

"Of course."

"But they're stupid!"

"Come on, Red, don't be so judgmental. You're just a pup, and you have so much to learn. A nice family will give you a good life. They'll love you, play with you, and spoil you. Knowing you have a good, safe home will lift a weight off my soul."

You think I listened? You've got to be kidding.
That's how I ended up in the military.

~

**Buy BECOMING K-9**